I0775476

No One Leaves
By
M. A. Savino

Warning:

This book contains multiple incidents of domestic violence and battery, which can trigger painful memories.

As a victim of past domestic violence, I know these pages may be difficult to read as much as they were for me to write. If you do not wish to continue, I understand.

The title, No One Leaves, is just a title. If you are in a dangerous situation, you can leave. Maybe not today or even tomorrow, but it is possible. There is hope.

Chapter One
Broken Record

My life used to be ordinary before I met Nick. His power and sex appeal sucked me in like quicksand, suffocating me. We spent all our spare time together for almost a year, then something happened.

Four months ago, I witnessed a horrible crime. A man had the life stomped out of him right before my eyes. People say eyewitness accounts can be unreliable, but that's not the case for me. I will never forget.

The police tracked down and interviewed everyone that ate dinner at the restaurant that evening, including me.

Nick wrapped his arm around me when the detective called me into the interview room and whispered in my ear.

"I trust you."

Those three words haunt me to this day. The way he said them sent chills from my neck to my toes. His tone was not angry or harsh, more like a warning to stay quiet without saying it. I'm not a good liar, but I did my best.

That night changed everything; it changed me. Knowing the limits of what I am willing to forgive and forget is important. What Nick did gave me nightmares for weeks after I snuck away. The time we shared came out of a storybook—the shopping sprees, fancy dinners, and cars are all gone now.

Leaving him had more downsides than material things. I abandoned everything and everyone and started over with less than I had when we met. To make matters worse, I don't feel safe without him or one of his cronies tagging along.

At first, I worked full-time, relaxed, and read books on the weekends. But living alone and paying for everything comes at a price I couldn't afford. So, I took a second job.

Stevie's Tavern isn't a dive but needs a woman's touch. The pain clinic I work for Monday through Friday supplies excellent medical benefits, but the pay is mediocre.

When I took the bartender position, I gave the owner stipulations. Everyone must pick up their messes. I'm not anyone's maid or mother. Nothing is worse than sticky floors and clutter resting on all visible surfaces. The place has the potential to be something great but lacks the vision to get it there.

Stevie doesn't care how I run things as long as my 'hotness' brings in more business. Blonde bartenders bring more male clientele, and having boobs is a plus. There must be something to it because the establishment's revenue has increased by fifteen percent since I started. Perhaps it had more to do with being sparkling clean than my presence behind the bar.

On an average weekend, I clear five hundred dollars nightly. Plunging tops and lacy push-up bras attract a ton of rich weirdos. But it isn't them who tip the most. The hardworking construction guys and blue-collar workers are the ones who appreciate me remembering their orders.

Friday nights are always busy. Everyone comes in complaining about their week. Only to return the following week and tell me again. It's an infinite loop of the same old song stuck like a skipping record, but I still listen as though it's my first time hearing their story.

One of my regulars, Beverly, an older woman with white shoulder-length wavy hair, plops her rotund frame down on her favorite stool. Before she speaks, I take a frosty cold glass from the freezer and pour her a pint.

Bev interlocks her fingers, rests her elbows on the unforgiving bar top, and sighs. "Thanks, Mia."

"Long day, Bev?"

"Long day, week, hell, this whole month has been a nightmare," she explains while chugging her entire beverage. "Another."

"Slow down, Bev. We don't need a repeat of last weekend."

Bev and another patron exchanged heated words that turned violent fast. Chaos ensued when the man refused to give up his seat to Beverly. She shoved him out of 'her' seat and dumped his Whiskey Neat on his head. Stevie ended up calling her a cab and making her leave.

A stool isn't private property, even if you do etch your name into it. Most of my regulars understand if a new person has taken their empty chair when they arrive. Beverly, on the other hand, is a creature of habit, and she gets jittery when anyone throws a monkey wrench into her routine.

"Mia, is everything all right?" Bev sets her second container down.

I sigh and force a smile. "Just a lot going on, that's all."

I do not care to address my concerns to the public, so I walk away from her and help another customer.

My foot sticks to the floor as I step on a circular red splatter. Stevie spilled the damn grenadine again and didn't wipe it up. I toss my cloth on the bar and slam the two-way door to the kitchen open.

"Stevie!"

"Jesus, Mia. Don't burst through the doors like the police. I almost shit my pants," he says, combing his blonde shaggy hair with his fingers.

"That's what happens when you spill something and don't clean it up," I steam.

"What? I didn't spill anything."

"Listen, don't play dumb with me just because you're the owner," I press.

"No, for real. I haven't left this room all night," he insists, raising his thick eyebrows. "Check the cameras."

"I plan on it after I take care of all of these people," I huff.

"Hey, Jerry getting hit by a car isn't my fault."

"Hire a temp, then. I don't like making people wait."

"Interviews are set up for Monday."

Same story, different day. Stevie has been putting off hiring, and I am tired of picking up all the slack. After his appearance on the news advertising his business, Stevie thinks he's God's gift to women.

The only problem is that Stevie isn't interested in any woman who ogles over him when they visit the establishment. He's fixated on me. I've expressed my desire to be single, but it didn't stop him from making a pass at me here and there. He's even gone as far as spilling something on his shirt and removing it in front of me to show off his washboard stomach.

Don't get me wrong, I love a six-pack, but Stevie is not my type. I've always dated men with dark hair and brown eyes. You know, the typical tall, dark, and handsome kind. Stevie is attractive, but he is my height and as pale as the white bathroom walls.

I think the real reason he hasn't hired anyone is because he likes to see me sweat. Not only that, but we work alone many nights. I imagine he fantasizes that one day I will give in, and he can throw me on top of the pool table and have his way with me—throwing his pool stick in my corner pocket. I shudder at the thought.

After buzzing through customer orders from left to right, I take a mop and scrub the gunk off the hardwood. My shoes squeak with every step, annoying me.

Bev waves a twenty-dollar bill at me from the other end of the room. I can't stand it when she does this. I'm not a stripper.

"Yes, Beverly?"

"Don't be stank young lady. This tip is a gift."

"What's the occasion?" Beverly isn't a huge tipper.

"Well, it's after midnight, so it's your birthday now, right?"

Shit. I forgot my birthday. Turning twenty-five isn't a milestone. Another patron raises his glass. I nod and raise my brows.

"Thanks for remembering, Bev. Another drink? My treat."

"Sure."

I stop in front of the man with his shot glass raised. His eyes are dark under his blue baseball cap. The undersides of his fingernails are filthy, as though he's been digging in the dirt.

"Another round?"

"No. I wanted to wish you a Happy Birthday, Mia."

I smirk and step away without responding. His tone and unspoken words hung in the space between us. I didn't intend on hanging around to listen to anything more he wished to say.

His eyes follow me to the other end of the room. From a distance, the black circles under his hat bore a hole through my face. My stomach quivered, and my hand poured an unsteady drink. It dribbles on the bar's mahogany surface, and I wipe it at once.

When I glance back over, the man is gone. A staggering breath escapes my lips as I swipe the sweat from my temple.

What a long, weird night.

Stevie appears from the kitchen at closing to help usher out the loiterers. After he locks the entrance, he pulls the shade down and turns to me.

"Mia. Is something wrong?"

Why is everyone asking me that? Can't a person have an off day? I continued cleaning the tables, ignoring him. The thing is, none of them are wrong. When something bothers me, I fall quiet. Even if I don't understand why, which isn't the case this time, I tell no one.

Lately, I sense someone watching me, but no one is behind me when I turn around. Perhaps working at Stevie's is making me paranoid. Many strangers come in and out all the time. Men and women ask me on dates, and I tell them I'm uninterested. My last relationship didn't end on a high note, and I am not ready to return to the dating game.

A few days ago, I found my cat dead in the front yard, devastating me. Tabitha, the orange tabby, was my only friend and companion. I adopted her after I moved here. She filled a gaping hole in my heart, and now she's gone. I blame the neighbor's stray. Tabitha couldn't make babies, but it didn't stop him from chasing her around like a horny teenager.

The neighbor said she thought a car ran her over, but I didn't notice any damage to Tabitha's body. She is probably covering for her fur devil. I cried for hours as I dug a pit and buried her in the back corner of the property. I bought a grave marker with a pawprint that reads, 'beloved friend.' My eyes water, and I dab them with a napkin from the table dispenser.

Stevie stops in front of me with his knuckles resting on his hips. "Hey, I'm not the one who spilled the grenadine. I swear."

"Fine. Prove it." I hiss, throwing the stained, white cotton rag at him, and walk toward the office.

He stomps in behind me and types a few strokes into his laptop. After scrolling for several minutes, his face changes.

"What the hell?" He squints at the screen and clicks his mouse.

"What?" I hustle to his side of the desk.

Words catch in my throat. The man in the blue hat is sprinkling grenadine on the floor. Stevie increases the speed of the video, and the man screws the top on and sticks it inside his coat.

"Bastard." I pound my balled-up fist onto the desktop.

"Like I said. I didn't do it," Stevie announced as he moseys out of the room.

Stevie can be mad all he wants, but he has butterfingers, so suspecting him first made sense. I stare at the still image of the man on the screen and wonder what I did to piss him off. Something about him is familiar, but I can't quite place him. I fold the computer shut and leave the office to help Stevie finish mopping the floors.

His half-hazard mop job left the air in the room stale and funky, so I poured cleaner straight onto the floor without diluting it and re-did it. A blister bursts on the inside of my thumb from the previous days shoveling. It drains down the wooden handle and stops when it loses momentum. I curl my fingers and gaze at the ruptured skin. Stevie rests his palm on my hand, covering the stinging hole.

"Mia, talk to me. What is wrong?"

I pull my hands away from him. Stevie, of all people, couldn't help me with my problem. I don't even know if the problem exists. It may be in my head, but that is not what my gut is telling me.

Chapter Two
Out of Place

The air in my house feels strange when I enter. I rub my arms as I sense someone's presence like they had just left, but their aura stayed behind.

Perhaps it's haunted. The owners rented it to me cheap after it didn't sell, so anything is possible.

I toss my keys in their bowl and plop down on the couch. Things are changing in subtle ways. Routine and order are essential to me, so I notice at once when something isn't where or how it should be.

Across from me, a book rests downward on its shelf. I squint, stand up slowly, and creep over to it. With my pointer finger, I tip it upright and press it into its rightful place.

Huh. I think to myself.

Reading is something I have little time for as of late. My bookshelf and the to-be-read list continue to grow, but there is only so much time in a day. One of these days, I am telling Stevie I need a weekend off before the shelf, or I break under pressure.

The bottle of alcohol I bought before work entices me from the dining room table. Why not? It's Friday night, technically Saturday morning, and I don't have to get up early, so I fill a stemless glass with strawberry wine.

The news is tragic, as always, so I turn the channel and watch an old sitcom instead.

My landline rings, and I ignore it. Calling someone at 3:00 a.m. is downright rude unless it is an emergency. The answering machine clicks, and I turn the TV volume down.

Dial tone.

That's what I thought. No doubt a wrong number anyway, especially this late.

My eyes flutter and struggle to stay open, so I shuffle my slipper-laden feet to my bedroom. The freshly washed comforter throws off a tropical scent as I tuck it under my chin and fall asleep.

A loud noise wakes me at 4:00 a.m. I slide a hunting knife out from in between my mattress and box spring and tiptoe down the hall. The kitchen window of the tiny house rattles on and off. I unbolt the door to the right of the fridge and peer into the darkness.

A stray cat jumps off the metallic trash can, tipping it over. Its sleek black coat disappears through a hole in the fence leading to the neighbor's yard.

"Dammit," I yell.

Orange and banana peels from yesterday's smoothie lie next to bloody tissues and various pieces of garbage.

Nose bleeds are something I've dealt with since childhood. Anytime the weather changes, the delicate interior skin of my nostrils split and bleed to no end.

After cleaning up the mess, I try and go back to sleep. My brain jumps from one thought to another like a frog on a lily pad, so I give up trying. I draw a hot bubble bath, strip off my pajamas, and lower my exhausted frame into the claw foot tub. The water encapsulates my body, reddening it with its heat. The faucet drips, leaking water onto my exposed toes. I sigh when I notice the pink chipping paint on my nails—time for another pedicure.

Manicures are a waste of money since I use my hands all day. Typing endless notes at the clinic wears the tips of my polish away. The pit in my stomach grew as I thought about work. After a fun-filled, entertaining weekend at Stevie's, the pain management job always dampens my mood. It is steady and secure but seeing patients in misery weighs on my soul. Some people do fake it, and I can always tell.

Snooping on social media and googling someone's name tells me a lot about the person before they arrive. Most cancel their appointments when I call and tell them we do not prescribe medications.

Some take their chances and show up regardless. My pace is fast, so I am skeptical when they follow me on my heels and say their pain level is a ten. Their pinpoint eyes and red noses give them away.

I try and stay in the present instead of worrying about the future. But the past is hard to shake as I float amongst the popping bubbles.

Memories crawl into my mind like a spider spinning its web. Around and around it goes until it reaches the bullseye in the middle. It's patient and waits to capture its food and devour it. That is how my last relationship was. Nick ran circles around me. He drew me in with his tangled web of deceit and sucked the sense out of me.

Whenever I spoke of leaving, he would talk me into staying. I do love him, but I'm afraid. He's never hurt me in any way, but when he's upset, his face and eyes turn dark. Everything about Nick is perfect. His sultry brown eyes, trimmed dark brown beard, tall stocky build, and charming personality made him irresistible to all the ladies, even me. But facial features and character aren't everything. Feeling safe is.

Nick handed me a rule book once, but I refused to open it. What family has rules anyway? Since I didn't care to read it, he offered up the most crucial rule. Being in 'the family is for life, and no one leaves.' So, when Nick asked me to marry him, I said yes, at first. But certain things can't be unseen, and boy, did I see a thing or two. So, the agreement to his proposal wasn't sincere. I did it to stall—time to gather my thoughts, pool my resources, and stash some cash.

I've changed since disappearing. I like who I am now, not the fragile, dependent side piece of Nick Castino, the family underboss.

There were perks to being his woman. I received endless gifts, protection, an apartment, and anything I could ever desire, but I didn't have him. Not all of him. He is still married. They separated, but that's not the point. How could he ask me to be his wife when he still belongs to someone else? He should have told me. I forgave him, but it wasn't just about betrayal.

I don't like secrets, and I don't tolerate cheating. Most of all, I like consistency. Nick's life is too unpredictable, and I soon discovered it could also be violent.

My stomach quivers as I remember the night I stumbled upon him and his men stomping the life out of a man who owed his family money. Blood shot into the air with every rise and fall of his foot. The person on the pavement's face no longer existed. His men tried multiple times to get him to stop and see me. But he was in a rage. He was stuck in the red zone in his mind, where violence and anger live until he's ready to use them. When Nick's eyes met mine, his fierce face softened. I think Nick knew at that moment that he had lost me.

A slight breeze floats under the bathroom door and chills my dangling arm—the kitchen door. I forgot to shut it all the way. Sometimes it sticks if I don't slam it hard and pops back open.

I yank a towel off its bar and wrap it around my dripping flesh. My feet leave a trail of moist footsteps on the oak floors. The door is ajar, as expected, but that's not all.

A bundle of roses with a little note card sits on the counter.

Happy Birthday, Mia.

My heart pounds fast as my eyes dart from one side of the room to the next. I paw through my kitchen drawer and take out a butcher knife. The back door creaks as it sways on the hinges. The cat from next door prances up to the open doorway. He peers inside, sniffs the air, and sticks his nose up before running away.

I grip the doorknob and slam the partition closed. A sliver lands on the ground in front of me. A few other bits of wood are on the floor near the underside of the entrance. I reopen the door and examine the strike plate for the lock. Gouges dig deep into the wood around it like someone jammed something in there. I didn't forget to close the door, as I thought. Someone

tampered with the door and left me this floral arrangement, and
I know who.

Chapter Three
Past

He found me. I don't know how, but he's here.

No one else would leave me flowers. My fists ball up before I seize the bushel and launch them into the wall.

"Nick?" I yell through the house as I investigate every room. "Come out, now."

But after an extensive search, the house is empty. Chills spread over the entire surface of my skin. This is ridiculous. Nick is playing games. No matter how many gifts he leaves me, I'm not taking him back.

The sun casts a sliver of light through my east-facing bedroom window. The day is starting without me. The towel around me slides to the floor as I rifle through my dresser. It's too early to dress for work, so I wear a pair of sweats, a T-shirt, and sandals. The cool morning air refreshes my lungs when I step outside and take a deep, cleansing breath.

Living upstate and away from New York City gave me a different perspective of the state. The Finger Lakes are home to many beautiful waterfalls and even more wineries. I want to do a wine tour, but going by myself is sad and boring. The annual festival is in July, and I can't wait to attend. It will give me a chance to meet new people and, with any luck, find a new favorite wine to drink.

An older man tips his hat and holds the door for me at my favorite coffee shop. It's abandoned inside. I tend to come later in the morning when people pack in here like sardines in a tin can. The barista raises her brows when she spots me.

"Wow. Someone is up early today." The girl smiles, handing me my caramel macchiato.

"Up, but not awake, that's for sure," I sigh as I stuff a dollar bill in her tip jar.

I sit by the window and read a newspaper left on the adjoining table. On the front page, a small article talks about a local woman who vanished a few days ago. The husband is crying in the picture at a news conference. In his hand is a missing person poster. The wife resembled me, which is creepy.

The police say he's not a suspect, but the husband did it nine times out of ten.

Knuckles thump the glass by my face startling me. Beverly waves at me through the shop window and plows through the door. How can someone who drinks as she does awaken with the birds?

"Morning, Mia," she says, sitting across from me.

"Morning."

The barista came from behind the counter and rested a black coffee before her.

"Any plans for today?" Bev asks as she slurps her cafe noir.

"No. I may have my toes done, but that's about it. Just another day to me."

Bev nods and gazes at the street when I excuse myself to use the restroom—the bathroom reeks of bleach and air freshener. My nose starts running as I sit on the toilet with my head in my palms. I want to enjoy my cup of energy in silence, but Bev is throwing off my day.

The door rattles with an insistent knock. Being a one-stall ladies' room is the only downfall of this place. After flushing and washing my hands, I open the door with a paper towel.

Bev leans on the wall by the doorway, waiting for me. "Mia, is everything all right?"

I roll my eyes and move past her. "I'm fine, thanks."

Bev swings her arms in front of her and stops at my table. The barista hustles beside her with a muffin. A burning candle flickers on top, melting wax onto the surface. The two burst out in song, and the morning crowd joins in.

My face reddens as they sing out of tune. I extinguish the flame with a quick, embarrassed breath, and the shop erupts in applause. Though I appreciated the gesture, I hate it when people focus on me.

After everyone goes back to their business, I turn to Bev. "What did I say? I said not a huge deal, remember?"

"Don't blame me. The barista is the one who approached me about it." She insists, wiping her lips.

"The barista? How did she find out about my birthday?" I whisper.

"Not sure. I've got to go, but I'm coming to Stevie's later." She grips my shoulder and squeezes it as she saunters away.

The barista returns to the table to pick up the mess Bev left. "Excuse me. How did you know about my birthday?"

"Some guy called and said he wanted today to be amazing. So romantic," she grins and strolls away.

She is oblivious. Nick does not do something for nothing. He's baiting me, and it has nothing to do with romance or love. It's about power.

My eyes dance around the exterior of the building. Nick's out there, somewhere, following me. My body jumps when glass shatters on the floor behind the register area. I rub my temples, toss a couple of dollars on the tablecloth, and leave.

The nail salon is a few storefronts down but doesn't open for another hour. I sit on the bench outside and take out my phone. My finger hovers over Nick's number.

If I call him, he wins, and I can't let that happen. Even though it's a new cell, I added him to my contacts. I made a clean break, but he would come if I needed him or was in danger. Right now, I want him to stop messing with my day.

A car horn beeps, startling me. I fumble, without success, to keep my cell from falling to the ground. When I lean down to grab it, a hand reaches it first. The man in the hat from the night before with dark, sinister eyes stoops before me. His gaze doesn't waiver from mine as he hands it to me without a word and rubs my thumb softly with his.

I have always heard of people being star-struck, but I never thought it was a real thing. As it turns out, it is. I open my mouth to speak, but fear keeps my words hostage. After several silent seconds, he stands, turns on his heels, and walks away from me. He's a handsome guy, but everything about him is unsettling.

"What the hell?" I murmur as my voice box returns to working order.

I planned to tell him off, but I couldn't do it. A tear escapes my lid, and I wipe it with my shaking hand. My frustration grows as the pounding in my head rises to intolerable levels.

The salon door pops open, and the nail technician waved me in with a smile, but I couldn't enter. I stare at her as if she has three heads. She does my pedicures regularly, so she isn't some stranger.

Routine. That's why this is happening. Everything I do is what I always do, making it easy for anyone to find me. I sprint down the sidewalk in the direction of home. I need to be more careful. Leaving Nick was for the best, but I know Nick doesn't like losing.

I glance over my shoulder multiple times, looking for Nick, his cronies, or the blue-cap man.

My phone dings, but I ignore it at first. I stop and examine a cute dress in a storefront window. It is pink with tiny white polka dots. I'd try it on if I weren't in such a hurry. My cell pings a reminder that I have an unread message. I ignore it as a stationary person in the reflection catches my attention. Across the street, standing in front of an insurance agency, a man resembling Nick watches me. My right palm grips the frame around the glass. I take several breaths and steady myself before gaining the courage to turn around and face him.

It's not him.

The man strolls across the street, diagonally, heading for a tailor shop beside the clothing store I am in front of. The resemblance is not even close. His hair is too light, and his face is too round. My eyes are playing tricks on me. I need to go home.

My phone vibrates in my hand—a reminder of the waiting text. I type in my password and click the green bubble.

Two words stopped my legs from moving and sent shockwaves through my trembling body as I read the message.

'Who's Nick?'

Chapter Four
Messages

The text came from an unknown number. No one has my information, so how did this person get it?

I thought about calling in to work. The problem is we are short-staffed, and Stevie makes terrible drinks. I gave him some lessons, but it didn't matter. He absorbs nothing.

Under the circumstances, I took a different route home. The machine blinks at me from across the room. Most people don't have phones, or an answering device connected to their houses, but I like having one. I kick off my shoes and walk over to it.

The red number on the screen alerts me to twenty messages. "What the…" Words catch in my throat.

No one ever calls me. Most of the time, the callers are spam or looking to extend my car warranty. My finger trembles over the play button. I draw in a deep breath and press it.

The first couple are hang-ups.

When I get to the third message, a man's voice speaks quietly and slowly.

'Happy Birthday, Mia.'

He continues breathing into the receiver for too long until finally hanging up.

My palms lean onto the end table the phone sits on. I debate continuing, but curiosity gets the best of me, and I cave, pressing the button.

'Fate brought us together like two separate roads joining and becoming one.'

I back away from the table and trip over the rug. My butt lands hard on the floor, and I crabwalk away. Who is this person? Is it the man from the sidewalk and bar? It didn't sound like him, but the echo of the machine could be altering his voice. I lean against the front of my accent chair. There are sixteen more messages, and I don't dare to listen to them. I want to know, but I don't.

The thick seat cushion gives me the leverage to stand. My legs struggle to move my frame forward. I pass the table, yank the cords from the machine, and toss it in the garbage outside.

The stray cat strolls along the top of the fence line. He stops, shoots me a judgmental glare, and jumps into the neighbor's yard.

"Little jerk," I say as I walk back inside.

No crime has been committed, so I can't call the police. Leaving non-threatening messages isn't against the law. Unless things escalate, there isn't much I can do.

The dark blue skinny jeans and red boat neck tank top I plan to wear to work lay across my comforter. I sit next to the outfit. Something less revealing may be in order. I should change if dressing provocatively lured this creepy guy into my life. He could be a crazed lunatic who's fixated on me. I'm not taking any chances.

I picked out baggy sweatpants, an oversized white T-shirt with the bar logo on the front, and canvas sneakers. The first elastic tie I try and put in my hair snaps and flies away, landing somewhere unknown. I sigh and grab another. After wrapping my hair in a messy bun, I cleanse my face clean of makeup.

I appear to have just climbed off a red-eye flight at the airport, but it's okay. Bird poop covers my black Scion TC's windows and mud cakes its wheel wells. I glance at my watch. There's time. I travel the short distance to the full-service automatic car wash and shift my vehicle into neutral. The worker nods, and my car jumps as it rolls into the building. Cloth tentacles flop on the glass like a fish out of water as rotating brushes scrub the sides.

Nick's face creeps into my head. I miss certain aspects of our relationship, but I don't miss his lifestyle. The man in the blue hat wouldn't stand a chance against Nick and his men. At least, I don't think he would.

The conveyer belt releases me from its grasp, and two men advance toward my car with yellow absorbent towels, quickly drying it. After giving each of them a couple of dollars, I turn onto the primary road and head to Stevie's.

The crowded lot makes parking by the entrance difficult. My body shudders at what I'm about to walk in on. If it's already this busy at five on a Saturday, it will be one hell of a night. When I whip the door open, a hoard of people breaks out in song.

Everyone I work with at the clinic, bar regulars, and Stevie all sing Happy Birthday. My face tingles and turns red as Stevie carries over a square vanilla frosted cake with rainbow sprinkles.

"Happy Birthday, Mia," Stevie grins and sets it on the bar before me.

I blow out the flaming wicks and force a halfhearted smile. "Thank you, everyone."

The doctor I work for walks through the crowd and passes me an envelope. He's not a man of many words and makes even fewer public appearances outside the clinic. So, the fact that he came meant the world to me.

On the back side of the bar, a pink box with black writing reads, '*Mia's birthday tips*.' I stuff the card from my boss inside and start making drinks for all my guests.

Bev stands beside a young clinical assistant who works with me, sitting in her chair. I shake my head. She will not cause a scene tonight or with someone I work with. I hand Bev a frosty glass of beer, and she winks. She's behaving, for now.

"What are you wearing? Since when do you dress like a bum?" Stevie asks, scanning my outfit up and down. "Don't get me wrong. You are hot in anything. It's just weird."

"Shut up and help me make some drinks."

"Don't get defensive. I'm just asking." Stevie says, putting his hands up.

"I felt like dressing comfortably, that's all." I lie.

Stevie gives me a slight nod, raises his eyebrow, and lets out a defeated breath. He knows I am holding something back but doesn't press further.

He bought several sheet pizzas for the crowd to consume and dozens of buttercream and chocolate frosted cupcakes. I planned to ask him if he handed out my number to anyone, but it wasn't necessary. Next to the phone on the wall near the kitchen, Stevie put up a list of important numbers. I've been after him since I started working here to make a list of emergency contacts, vendors, and employees. I didn't notice it the night before. It's written in black marker on white notepaper so anyone with a keen eye can see it from far away. He didn't even put the numbers in order or categorize them. They are a jumbled disorganized mess, just like Stevie. I tore the paper from its tack, folded it in half, and stuffed it inside my card box. What a dipshit, I think to myself. Any normal person would know not to put employee personal information in public view. He might as well have written it on the wall in the men's room.

I toss my napkin and paper plate in the trash and head to the restroom. A couple of bar patrons glance at me as I pass them. They giggle their way out the front door and disappear. One of the ladies' room stalls has an out-of-order sign, and the other has a broken lock. I push my palm against the chipped partition to hold it closed.

Graffiti provides me with something to read as I conduct my business. The door swings open as I release it to wipe. It creaks slowly away from me, opening the stall. Anyone who came through the door at that moment would have a clear view of me sitting on the throne, and so would everyone inside the bar. On the wall, in a gray permanent marker, is a message meant just for me.

For a good time, call Mia…

My home number is beneath the message. Why would a woman post such a thing? I don't know anyone here. Not really. I wipe fast, wash my hands, and open the bathroom door. Stevie furrows his brows as I shove the men's room door open. A clinic employee glances over his shoulder at me as he relieves himself at the urinal.

"Mia, I think you're in the wrong restroom." He whispers, zipping up his pants.

"Sorry, I know. I need to check something."

"Well, I won't get in your way."

He yanks the handle and exits without washing his hands. *Gross.* I need to speak with my boss on Monday about having a meeting on proper hand washing. I hope he didn't get me a card.

The stall door is greasy to the touch, and my stomach turns queasy. My sneaker slips on a slimy substance on the floor, and I stifle a scream. Bits and pieces of used wet toilet paper surround the toilet. It's caked on the seat, and around the base. The inside holds a massive amount of feces. I ran out of the space and vomited in the sink. I didn't even have a chance to check the walls for my information. It wasn't necessary. Written on the bathroom mirror, in permanent marker, was another message.

'Mia is hot, and I want to stuff my cock in her. If you do too, call her.'

Beneath the message is my phone number. Multiple people added to it. Someone even drew a penis pointing at a butthole. Others just wrote, '*me too*,' next to the primary drawing.

"Pigs," I say to the empty room.

The door opens a crack, and Stevie sticks his head in. "Hey, are you planning on being here for long? I have a line of people needing drinks, and some men need to use the bathroom."

"Stevie, the toilet is clogged, and I'm not cleaning it." I point to the message above the sink. "Did you know about this?"

"Now, Mia, you know I use my private office bathroom."

"That is not what I asked you, Stevie. Did you know?"

"Know what?

"About this shit," I yell, grabbing him by the sleeve and pulling him in front of me.

His eyes widen as he reads over the vulgar words. "I don't come in here, Mia. And if I did, I would certainly have cleaned this. I'm so sorry. I will stick an out-of-order sign on the door and paint it after closing."

"You better," I insist and storm out of the room.

Why do men feel the need to speak in such a way about women? Do they think it makes us want them? If anything, it turns us off and makes us want to punch them in the face. I know someone I'd like to hit, the person who wrote the message. The handwriting in the men's and women's room appears to be the same. How could they have gone into both without anyone noticing? The bar cameras only face the patrons. There are none in the hallways. Even if there were, you wouldn't be able to tell who or when it occurred with all the foot traffic. I didn't use the bathroom the night before, we were too busy, and I held it until I got home. For all I know, it could have been last night, tonight, or last weekend. But with the number of messages I came home to, I have no doubt that someone did it last night.

Chapter Five
Cards

Stevie and I ushered the last patrons out the front door just after one. The stalker didn't appear—a welcome gift.

After cleaning all the tables, I broke the silence between us.

"Stevie, someone called my house, and I think they got my number from here."

"I'm sorry. I'll take the list down, paint the bathroom and clean the mirror."

"I'd appreciate it. Employee numbers can be in your office filing cabinet and vendors and emergency responders in public view. I have the list, and I plan to redo them on my computer."

"Thanks, Mia. I am sorry. What did the person say?"

"He wished me a happy birthday and said something about fate bringing us together. Then I had a bunch of hang-up calls."

Stevie rested his hands on the bar. His long fingers drum the surface in rhythm. He shakes his blonde hair and blows an exaggerated breath at the ceiling.

"I didn't mean to upset you," he says, resting his palm on mine.

I slide my hand out from under his. Stevie means well, but his passes are getting annoying. Besides the constant need to touch me, he's disorganized, flighty, and irresponsible. Stevie is everything that drives me crazy packed into one human.

"It's okay. Please take care of the graffiti tonight."

"I have some extra paint in the backroom. I'll clean it this evening. You have my word."

"Thanks. Can you pass me my birthday box?" I say, pointing behind him.

"Sure. I put a card in there too."

"Thanks, Stevie, for everything."

"No problem," he grimaces.

Perhaps he expected a thank you kiss. *Yuck.* A tiny amount of bile creeps into my throat at the thought.

The box is heavier than it appears. I placed it next to me in the car and debated whether to open it now or at home. Stevie taped every crease and edge. My aunt did this when I was a child at Christmas. My cuticles would bleed as I picked at all the edges, trying to find an opening. Either she didn't like me, or it was some kind of lesson in patience.

I'll need scissors or a knife. Stevie only left a slit at the top to push cards through.

Idiot. I sigh, stick my key in the ignition, and turn. Nothing. I try again—still nothing.

"What now?" I rest my head on the steering wheel.

Stevie appears next to my window, making me jump. I opened the car door and shoved him.

"Don't sneak up on me, Stevie."

"Sorry. What's the matter? Won't it start?"

"No. I don't know what's wrong with it."

"Well, hop in my car, and I'll take you home." He smiles as he points at his pickup. "I can check out your car in the morning when it's light outside."

The awkward drive to my place made me second-guess his offer for a ride. He's not a stranger, but we work together, and letting him take me home feels too personal.

Stevie turns too fast into my driveway, just missing the neighbor's cat.

"Jeepers. Slow down," I yell at him.

He raises his hands and shrugs. "It's just a cat, Mia. Want me to walk you inside?"

My pitch-black, lightless house rattles me. I don't want to go in alone. If it were anyone else, I would have said yes. Inviting Stevie in is not something I am comfortable with.

"Thank you for the offer, but I'm fine. Goodnight, Stevie."

I peer through the blinds and watch him back out into the street. His tires squeal as he kicks it into drive and takes off toward the bar.

The living room is too dark to see, but something feels off, and it's not the first time. Someone has been here. I can feel it. The slight scent of cologne fills my nostrils when I sniff the air.

"Hello?... Nick?"

Nothing. I flick the light switch on with my thumb and drop the card box. Across the room, multiple books rest on their ends. The answering machine I threw away is back on the table next to my reading chair. I couldn't move. My body plasters itself against the painted drywall with my hand still on the switch. It melts to the floor like ice cream on hot pavement. I reach into my sweats, take out my cell, and call the police.

When they arrive, I'm still sitting on the floor. The officer crouches and takes off his hat.

"Ma'am, what seems to be the problem?"

"Someone came into my house, turned down my books, and the machine was in the trash, and now it's back."

"Why did you throw it out?"

"Someone left me a bunch of messages. I didn't listen to them all, but they were unsettling."

"Okay. We are going to do a walkthrough. Stay here."

He and his partner enter one room after another and shake their heads. The first officer who spoke to me stood beside the answering machine and hit play.

'You have no messages.'

Whoever came into my house, has erased all the evidence. The second officer stares at the misplaced novels and pushes them upright one at a time using his pen.

'I-S-E-E-Y-O-U.'

"What did you say?" I asked him as I stood.

"The out-of-place ones. The first letter in the title of each book spells out, *'I see you.'* Does anyone else have access to your home?"

"No. It's only me." My arms hug my waist.

The first officer takes out his notepad.

"Ma'am, there isn't a lot to go on here. If you believe someone is messing with you or coming inside, get some cameras. Did you change the locks when you moved in?"

"No."

"You should. It could be a former owner or someone who still has a key. Here's my card. If anything else happens, don't hesitate to call."

"Thanks. I'll be sure to throw your card at the guy when he comes back to murder me," I grimace.

"There is no evidence anyone has been here besides your turned-down books. We may have something to work with if a neighbor or you see someone."

"Fine. Whatever," I sigh and cross my arms.

After they left, I picked up the box from the floor and set it on the coffee table. The scissors in my junk drawer have stamps stuck to their blade. One of these days, I'll clean it out. I stick its sticky blade through the slot and cut the entire top off. Piled high inside are money, cards, and personal customer notes from customers. I sort them into two stacks—the cards in one and the money in the other.

First, I count the cash. Five hundred and seventy-four dollars and twelve cents. *Not bad.* Next, I open the cards. Some are empty with well wishes, but most have a check or money. The last one has two tarot cards inside, Death and The Devil.

I drop them and scoot away. My hand slides to the card, and I open it using my pointer and middle finger.

'Happy Birthday, Mia. See you soon.'

There is no signature, only a smiley face. I rip it into tiny pieces with shaking hands, snatch the box and throw it across the room. My cell phone sits on the floor by the door. I grabbed it and searched for Nick's number. Once again, I can't call. I seize the policeman's number, start dialing, then stop. A birthday card and some tarots are not enough.

Tomorrow I'm buying cameras. It's the only way to find out who is coming and going as if they live here.

Chapter Six
Surveillance

Sunday is my favorite day of the week. I can clean my house, run errands, sit in my pajamas all day, or work in my yard.

Not today, though. I'm driving to the local hardware store to buy security cameras instead.

The driveway is empty when I step out of the house and stop. My Scion is still sitting at Stevie's.

"Dammit," I say to the cloudy sky.

The older woman who lives next door is rocking in her creaking chair on her front porch. She's wearing a thin white nighty and pink slippers, petting the annoying cat who keeps getting in my garbage. Satan's sidekick stares at me with its green eyes as she strokes its smooth, onyx back.

"Someone steal your car?" she says, lifting her glasses.

"No. It's at the bar."

"Huh… Want a lift?"

"Yes. Thank you, Mrs. Baxter."

Most people would have put on some clothes before they leave the house. However, Mrs. Baxter enters the house and returns with her purse and keys.

The sun hits her nightgown when she steps off her stoop, revealing nothing underneath. Her frame crosses over from the driver's side to unlock the passenger door, confirming my suspicion. I divert my eyes when her breasts pop out of her gown.

"Sorry about that, dear. The girls have a mind of their own sometimes," she giggles.

I stay quiet beside her. Even though we have been neighbors for several months, I barely see her. Having two jobs keeps me away most days. And when I am home, I want to either sleep or lie down and relax.

The primary road is congested with traffic. Mrs. Baxter floors her Buick and weaves in and out of the obstacles like a Nascar driver. My hand grips the 'holy shit' handle as she barrels around a corner and slides across the gravel into Stevie's lot. Dust kicks up in the air and floats into a group of patrons smoking outside. They throw their hands up, and she waves at them.

"Thanks, Mrs. Baxter," I say, rushing to exit.

"Anytime, neighbor."

Mrs. Baxter spins her tires, shooting stones in every direction, as she peels out of the parking lot. People scatter as pebbles fly at them. Stevie comes rushing out and gawks at a window beside his front door. A tiny pebble lodges itself in the center of a star-shaped shatter on its pane.

"What is going on? What happened to my window?" Stevie yells, pointing at the growing crack.

"My neighbor gave me a ride. She's kind of nuts."

"Kind of? She damaged my property."

"Stevie, where is my car?"

"Out back. A wire on the battery came loose, so I fixed it."

"Thanks. Any idea how it happened?"

Stevie turns with a spacey stare, shaking his head. "Not sure. Come on. The keys are behind the bar."

Stevie yanks the door open, storms inside, and scoops my keys out of the 'too drunk to drive bowl.'

"Want to stay a couple of hours to help today? This tournament is hopping."

"Not a chance. Sundays are my only day off, and I have things to do."

"Fine." Stevie pouts, grabbing a roll of tape.

From the corner of my eye, the blue hat stalker is eyeing me from a pool table as he shakes someone's hand.

"Stevie, what the hell is he doing here?" I say, nodding in the direction of the tournament floor.

"Listen, he paid to participate, and I am not about to lose money over some prank."

"A prank? Stevie, you should have banned him or said something to him after he messed with me."

"If you were my girl, I would have," Stevie smirks as he wanders away.

I'm no idiot. Stevie lacks the courage to confront anyone, even if I were his girl. He's all talk, no action.

"Mia, he apologized for the mess," Stevie announces as he returns to me.

"Oh, and that makes everything better?"

"Well, no, but if it makes you feel any better, I think he likes you," Stevie grins as he sets a drink before me. "He asked me to give this to you as a peace offering when you come in."

"Not funny," I huff as I slide it away. "I'm not interested in being friends."

"Suit yourself," he says as he tosses the clear liquid down his throat.

I gaze at the pool tables to give the prankster the middle finger, but he's gone. My eyes scan the room, looking for him.

When I turn around, a shot glass filled with golden liquid is in his outstretched arm. Before he has a chance to speak, I smack the offering, splashing it on his face.

How dare he think he can win me over after tarnishing my nice, clean floors?

My blood simmers as I spin on my heels and leave without looking back. My car turns over on the first try, so I drive the few miles to the hardware store.

They carry an enormous selection of cameras. As I walk down the concrete aisles, a man in an orange vest approaches me with his arms behind his back. My instinct is to back away. Just because he has a uniform does not mean he works here. Anyone can sneak into a breakroom and take one. The man's demeanor is nervous, and now so am I.

"N... need some help?" The associate asks with a stutter, letting his hands fall before him.

They're empty, and I blew an upward breath, shifting my side-swiped bangs. His altered speech makes him self-conscious, hesitant, and awkward.

Now I know he's not a killer, I drop my shoulders, and I speak confidently. "I want something easy to install and to use."

He picks up a white box with a four-pack of surveillance equipment and passes it to me.

"This one is w... wireless, and the charge l... l... lasts about three months. Just n... need a drill, and a l... ladder."

"A stepladder I have but not a drill. Any on sale?"

"Sure. R... right this way," he smiles and signals me to follow him.

Two hundred and fifty-six dollars later, I'm on my way home. For the first time in several days, I relaxed. My street is bustling with people working on their lawns, so I start inside the house first.

The step stool from the storage shed smacks into the wall as I round the corner leaving a triangle-shaped ding. The camera in the living space faces the bookcase area and dining room. Putting up the first one and connecting it to my cell phone takes less than ten minutes. The clarity is excellent.

I move on to the bedroom and place the second one in my closet. Some may say it is an inappropriate location, but I am not taking any chances. If someone sneaks in and murders me, the police will have a recording.

The last two go at the front and back entrances. This nonsense has wasted half of my day, but I still have some time to relax before bed. I grab a book, and glass of wine, and sit in my cozy chair—five minutes into reading, the phone rings.

"Argh."

The novel falls to the floor when I stand up. The cord comes right out of the wall with a violent twist of my wrist. I'm done with calls, interruptions, and, most of all, stalkers. If someone wants to talk to me, they can come here and be on camera.

I sink back into the cushion and continue reading. Scratching comes from the front entrance, and the page in my hand crumples under my grasp.

"Grrrr…" I growl as I toss my hands in the air and gaze at the ceiling. "Why can't I just have a normal, quiet day?"

The scratching grows more intense as I narrow the gap between myself and the door. I take my cellphone from my pocket and open the camera app. Sitting at the door is a tiny, long-haired tiger kitten. As if it knew I was watching, it peered at the camera and let out a pitiful *'meow.'*

I cast the door aside and kneeled to it. "Poor baby. Are you okay?" I say as I scoop it into my arms.

When I turn it over to check the gender, a collar falls to the floor. The white-bearded tiger cat is a girl.

"I'm naming you, Lady, after the Bearded Lady," I say, scratching behind her silky ears and kissing her fluffy head.

She purrs in my arms as I reach down and pick up the collar. The pink neckwear is new, but the name tag is old. It falls to the floor in slow motion when I read the name.

Tabitha.

Chapter Seven
Too Quiet

My tears of joy turn from sadness to shock. I carry the furball with me to the backyard. Fresh dirt sits outside the once-covered hole in the corner where I buried my feline friend.

Flies buzz around the gaping pit, and the scent of decay floats from its depths. I set the kitten in the tall grass beside Tabitha's grave. Although it isn't the kitten's fault, I still cast an angry glare of hatred upon it.

Someone has dug up my furry companion, removed her nametag, and put it on this imposter's neck. The baby lets out a throaty cry from the depths of its hungry throat. I don't want to keep her, but I won't let her starve. I stare over my shoulder at Mrs. Baxter's back porch. She is a suitable pet parent despite her skimpy attire.

I walk around the front of her house and tap on the glass door. Mrs. Baxter answers with a head full of tight pink curlers in her hair and a purple robe.

"Oh, my goodness. Did you get a new baby girl?" She squeals as she takes the furry animal from me.

"No. I found her by my door, and I'm not ready to be a cat mom again," I say, stroking the kitten's soft spine. "Could you take her in?"

She presses the bearded tiger to her face and talks to her with intermittent cat noises. The kitten licks Mrs. Baxter's nose, which seals the deal. "She loves me," she proclaims and carries her inside.

"So, is that a yes?" I ask, walking into her dark, curtain-drawn living room.

"Well, how could I say no? She has such a cute face." Mrs. Baxter says as she tips the kitten's chin up to the ceiling. "I think I'll call her Georgia. Doesn't she look like a Georgia?"

"She sure does," I smile. "Mrs. Baxter, what's that smell?"

"Oh, shit, I forgot about the cookies. Honey, let yourself out."

She disappears down the hallway with Georgia chasing after her. In my head, I hoped she would offer me a fresh-baked cookie. Instead, she tosses me out like an inconvenience despite bringing her a new best friend.

I hustle down her stairs and back to my house. The collar still sits on the floor where I dropped it. I pick it up and carry it back to Tabitha's final resting place. After mourning my cat for the second time, I fill the tub, drip in some lavender oil, and pour a tall glass of wine. The dirt on my hands and knees lifts off my skin and disappears under the surface.

I rest my forearm across my eyes. How can someone be so cruel and vindictive as to dig up a dead animal so they can mess with me? Nick may have one of his soldiers do it, but this didn't feel like him. I reach for my phone and open the camera application. Whoever dropped the kitten off managed to avoid the surveillance equipment. You only see a gloved hand resting the kitty on my stoop.

The phone slips from my grasp and plunges into the suds. "Dammit," I huff, fumbling under the surface for it.

It has a water-resistant cover, but I don't take any chances. I hoist myself out of the tub but can't find my towel, so I walk naked into the kitchen to find rice. As I seal my phone in a rice filled Ziplock bag, I sense someone staring at me across the yard. Mrs. Baxter smiles and waves from her kitchen window. I return the pleasantry and scurry out of the kitchen with reddening cheeks.

Not only is the towel that hangs in my bathroom gone, but all of them are missing from my linen closet. "What the fuck." I announce to the empty space. If I call the police, they'll say it's a prank or nothing to worry about. Towel theft isn't exactly a top priority.

I'm tired of these twisted mind games. Allergy medicine sits unopened on my dresser. I consider taking the whole damn bottle as more than enough falls into my palm, but I think better of it and only take the two as directed.

After an eventful Sunday and a pleasant night's rest, I should have predicted Monday would be a shit show. Somehow an addict slipped into our building and threw herself on the floor crying in pain. When I approached the chaos, I recognized her from the bar and called her.

"Joan, let's not play these games. Perhaps a little time in rehab would be beneficial."

She stops yelling, and her head cranks in my direction like a possessed demon. The disparity in her eyes gave me a hint to move, but I didn't react in time. Joan grabs my shirt with one hand and punches me with the other.

The clinic trains all its employees to remain calm. But my reflexes didn't match my training, and I struck her back. Crimson liquid shoots out of her nose and splatters on the wall beside us.

The doctor I work for seizes me under the arms and drags me into his office. Two clinical aids subdued Joan until the police arrived. Human Resources orders me to take the rest of the day off pending an investigation, but home is not where I want to be.

I catch a glimpse of my reflection in the rearview mirror. The side of my face is swelling and turning colors as I pull into a shopping center for retail therapy. Despite my boss's small ice pack, a shiner is developing on my cheekbone.

My hands shake as adrenaline surges through every vein in my frustrated body. Not because I'm scared but because I'm angry. Everything and everyone are contributing to my anxiety. What I need is peace.

A woman exits the clothing place with two overfilled bags. Her husband rolls his eyes as he pops the trunk of their white Cadillac so she can load them in. She grins at me, and I nod when the woman gives me two thumbs up.

I mustered up the energy to leave my car and enter the building. Now I understand her excitement. Every rack has a sign reading, 'at least fifty percent off everything.' After grabbing the last cart, I rifled through the shelves for hours.

There is a sign on the dressing rooms. Since all sales are final, the store is keeping them closed to the public. If none of these fit, they are mine to keep.

Ultimately, I left with five new outfits and saved one hundred and thirty dollars. I throw my haul into the backseat, lock the doors, and head to the coffee shop.

The shortcut between the library and the store is brick and lined with various flowers. I stop, pluck a red daylily, and stick it in my hair. Despite starting shitty, my day is looking much better.

Floral scents fill the air as I round the corner and spot the man in the blue hat. He walks toward me with fast-moving legs, and I back away just as fast. My body smacks hard into the wall as his palms slap on either side of my head.

He doesn't touch me at first. Instead, he plants his knee between my thighs without touching them and fixes his eyes on mine. I turn my head away, and he turns it back. Fear keeps me from fighting or objecting to his proximity. A transparent force coming from him keeps me there. Like opposing magnets, we float invisibly to everyone around us. No one who came by said anything or interceded. They walk by and mind their business. The man's tan hand comes away from the wall, and I cower, expecting the worst.

He touches the bruise on my cheek with a soft tenderness I didn't expect.

A tear travels from my lid and meets his fingertip. His other hand leaves the brick, and he encapsulates my face in his palms.

He swipes my quivering mouth with his thumbs and whispers. "I'm sorry for everything that has happened, and for what's to come."

I want to...no need to ask him what he's talking about. My voice box is like a concrete block in my throat. Nothing came out when I parted my lips. Air staggers from his nostrils as though he's struggling. The man removes the flower from my hair, inhales its scent, and strolls away.

I hold my breath until my chest starts to ache. My body sways, and I collapse into the landscaping, knocking the trapped wind out of my lungs. I stay where I land, lying in the bed of annuals, hyperventilating. Stars dance before my eyes as oxygen struggles to reach its destination.

A passerby calls to me from the sidewalk. Her voice is far away, and I don't respond at first when she stoops in front of me.

"Want me to call for help?"

"No. I'm fine," I lie and take her hand.

My legs jiggle as I find the strength to lift off the ground and trudge out of the alley. Darkness is descending on my life. It wraps around me like a weighted blanket, suffocating me. Why is this man tormenting me? His touch is tender and kind, but his actions are those of a madman hell-bent on scaring the literal piss out of me.

When I return, the store is dark inside, and my vehicle is the last to leave. A droplet lands on my forehead as I cry against the hood.

Is this man a test? Did Nick send him to torment me? Does he want to harm me?

My fists pound the car over and over until a dent appears. A puddle of earthly water slowly encapsulates me as the storm cloud bursts above me. I gaze at my knuckles. Joan is the first person I have ever punched, and I enjoyed doing it.

Rain pours over me as I raise my face to the heavens with my mouth open. The weight of my drenching clothes pulls me to the ground. The puddle beneath me becomes deeper and deeper. Perhaps a priest will wander by and baptize me. Who am I kidding? Nothing will help the dents in my Scion, my current situation, or anything else that may come about. The squished bugs on my windshield are all the storms can help me with.

The way things are going, it would take a miracle or act of God to turn my day around. Something more substantial is in order.

I need a drink or two. Okay, maybe ten, and I know where to find one.

Chapter Eight
Trashed

The green painter's tape on Stevie's window resembles an asterisk. It will no doubt remain broken for months or even years from now. Stevie doesn't like paying for anything.

I whip the door open and plop my frustrated rear end on a barstool next to Beverly. She leans away from me and shakes her head.

"Well, well, look who decided to join us." She scoffs.

"Don't start. I am not in the mood, Bev."

Stevie drops a glass before me and over-pours his best tequila. I toss it down my throat and flip it over. The fiery fluid burns its way into my empty stomach.

"Mia, what happened?" Stevie asks as he turns my face, and I let him.

"Unruly patient. I need a rum and Coke and some loaded tater tots."

"I'm on it," Stevie announces and disappears into the kitchen.

Bev strolls to the left of me. She examines the shiner on my cheek and furrows her brow. "Whose butt needs kicking for this?"

"No one. An illness is an illness, no matter what kind it is. The person who did this requires treatment. End of story."

She nods her head and returns to her seat. Stevie crashes through the two-way door with a massive pile of fried potatoes with mounds of bacon and cheese. On the side sits two containers of ranch and a fork. I shove the utensil away and use my fingers. Seconds later, my drink arrives. Bev eyes my plate, and I slide the food in her direction.

"I'll never eat them all. Have some."

An enormous grin spreads across her face, and her eyes light up. "Thanks, Mia."

She dives into the center instead of eating what's closest to her. Her nail beds are filthy and dampen my appetite.

Stevie is drying a glass when something grabs his attention by the door. I twist my head, and two beautiful blonde women wearing sparkling party dresses stagger into the bar. I smirk as they use each other as leverage to stumble their way to the bathroom.

Laughter echoes through the stalls of the ladies' room, and Stevie and I shake our heads—college girls. One of them could be me if I ever finished. I was only one semester shy of graduating with my bachelors in nursing when I met Nick.

He launched a metal rod in my gears of motivation, and I never went back. I work two jobs now to keep the utilities on and repay student loans. School is expensive, and so is living. My relationship with Nick took more than my career.

When my father found out I didn't return because of him, he chucked all my belongings into the street. My mother is deceased. So, with nowhere to go or money to speak of, Nick rented me an apartment. Perhaps it was his plan all along. I was indebted to him.

The girls appear from the restroom with red cheeks. They shuffle to the wall-mounted jukebox and make a few selections. Glass clanks against the wooden bar as Stevie places another drink in front of me.

"This one is on me," he grins.

"Thanks, Stevie."

I smile at the golden liquid and take out my phone. I've never called off work before. But after my day, I deserve it. My boss answers at once and says it's not a problem. I scoop the liquor up and chug it.

Beverly places her palm on my arm and squeezes it. "Mia, how about we call a cab."

My head bobbles a little, and I raise the glass and slam it back onto the bar. "I'm no quitter. Stevie, bring me another."

Bev shakes her head at him, and he shrugs his shoulders. Another drink manifests in front of me, and I don't recall drinking it. One minute it was there, and the next gone. The girls who came to use the bathroom are now dancing to a song they selected. I'm a lightweight with alcohol and know better, but I threw back another shot and joined them.

A few lingering men came out on the dance floor as well. Sweat rolls down the back of my scrubs, and my hair topples out of its bun. The lights flash different colors, and the floor vibrates under our feet through multiple songs. One man spun me several times in a circle. With every turn I made, I became more unsteady.

My mouth is watering, and I sway away from them. Stevie reaches for me as I pass the bar heading for the door. Once outside, I hurl partially digested tater tots into the bushes. The guy who twirled me places his palm on my lower back.

"Don't touch," I ask.

The man removes his hand from my spine and strokes my ass. "Come on, baby. Why don't you let me take you home?"

"I said, get off me," I screamed and shoved him.

"Bitch," he hisses and shoves me back, hard.

I would have landed on the ground if it weren't for the man in the blue ball cap. He catches and swings me behind him in one smooth motion. His face is clean-shaven, and a musky cologne fills my nostrils when his flannel shirt shifts. He lets me go and delivers a harsh punch to the man, knocking him unconscious.

I wobble to my car, take my fob from my pocket, and hit the unlock button. When my hand reaches the driver's side door, the man in the hat snatches the keys.

"Give me my keys, you shit," I slur.

"No," he says, holding them above my head and out of reach. "You're not driving drunk."

I jump into the air and try to take them back without success. He grins as I make a second attempt and miss. I smack him across the face, wiping his smile away. His eyes widen and roll as he exhales an annoyed breath simultaneously.

Preparing for the worst, I cover my face with my arms when he approaches. He seizes me around the waist, scoops my belligerent ass up, and loads me into the back seat. I try to push the door open with my feet, and he stuffs them back in and shuts the door. The man climbs behind the driver's seat, adjusts my mirror, and turns the car on. He's taking me. What have I done? I don't know why I hit him. I remember how good it felt to smack the shit out of Joan. Perhaps I wanted to feel good again. But this is different. This man has done nothing but stalk me and make my life hell. So, why am I not afraid when I should be? Alcohol has made me brave.

I run my yap behind him as he drives out of Stevie's lot.

"This is kidnapping and theft of my body." I slur.

"I'm taking you home, Mia." His palms squeeze the steering wheel as he blows out a loud, drawn-out breath. "You're so beautiful," he whispers.

"You killed my cat, didn't you?" I spit, ignoring his comment. "Murderer."

"I love cats. I would never hurt them," he insists.

Oh, that's so sweet he's a cat lover like me. Well, except for Mrs. Baxter's demonic furball. He's an asshole. What am I doing? Wake up, Mia. This man is not a nice guy just because he likes felines and says you're pretty. Did he just say he's taking me home? Think, Mia…think.

"Wait, how do you know where I live?"

My eyes lock with his in the rearview mirror, and his face blurs. The next thing I remember is lying in bed. My muscles have no strength to fight. If he wants to take me as I am, he could, but he doesn't. Instead, he covers me to my neck and swipes my hair from my face.

"Who are you?" I whisper as he caresses my cheek.

Silence is the only response as the room spins around me, and my eyes refuse to stay open. The floor creaks as quiet footsteps fade away, and so do I.

Chapter Nine
A Name to the Face

A headache from the depths of hell wakes me at ten in the morning. My scrubs stick to my sweaty, confused flesh like Velcro.

The fan hums above me as I struggle to remember the night before. My phone rings in the living room, and I roll my eyes. The pressure in my bladder is intense, so I force myself up.

My forearm smacks into the door frame as I fumble down the hall toward the bathroom. I reach the toilet, bounce off its surface, and land on the floor.

"Ohhhhh…my head," I groan at the ceiling.

After my first attempt to plant my ass on the toilet fails, I refocus all my energy into trying again, this time succeeding. The phone chimes again, and I stop midstream.

Someone must have plugged it back in. I finish peeing and fly out of the room like a mad woman, tripping my way into the living room. Next to the ringing annoyance is a note, two white oblong pills, and the blue baseball hat.

Mia, take these and drink lots of water.
Tony.
P.S. Answer the phone.

As if on cue, it rings a third time and this time, I answer.
"Hello?"
No one responds.
"Tony?"
'Who the fuck is Tony, Mia?'
Nick's voice catches me off guard. Words stutter out of my mouth as I try and explain.
"I don't know. I…"

Inaudible explicit screams fill my ear as I panic and hang up. The telephone starts again seconds later, so I yank it out of the wall, taking the cover with it. This time, I smashed it to bits on the table. I ran to my room and seized my cell from the dresser. There are several missed calls from Stevie, the pain clinic, and an unknown number. None of them are from Nick.

I open the camera app and check all captured activity for the last twenty-four hours. The only thing on the recording is the man I now know is Tony, bringing me home. I fast forward to after I fall asleep and see where he goes. Tony's writing the note and removing his hat. The hair underneath is jet black, cut in a neat fade with a hardline. Tattoos peek out from his T-shirt on both arms. I zoom in on his left arm. It's an Italian flag. Perhaps this is why he's here. Nick sent him.

The suitcase on the top shelf of my closet slams to the floor as I pull it down. The safest thing to do is leave. My hands move fast as I stuff as much as possible into the luggage and shoot out the front door. I stop short when a woman carrying a bouquet of red roses strolls up the sidewalk with a massive smile.

"Someone is about to have an amazing day," she screeches.

Her voice is a cross between nails on a chalkboard and two cats ready to fight over territory. She hands me the flowers and blows a single note on a harmonica.

"No. Don't you dare. I don't want to hear a single note come from your mouth." The woman's smile turns upside down as I shoo her off my stoop. "Just give me the notecard and be on your way."

The singing florist removes a white card from her shirt pocket with her pointer and middle fingers and flicks her wrist as she passes it to me. I keep my eyes on her as she hums back to her delivery van and rolls slowly away. The card's message is short and sweet.

'Feel better soon.'
Tony

His capitals are tall when he writes, adding a bit of flare and sophistication. My handwriting resembles a doctor writing on a script pad in a hurry. It's messy, disorganized, and barely legible. The flowers are a sweet gesture that I can't accept.

Mrs. Baxter whips into her driveway as I rest the bouquet on the roof of the car and stuff my bags into the trunk. She rolls her driver's side window down and yells at me. "Where are you going in such a hurry?"

"Vacation."

"Sounds like fun. Georgia says, hi," she smiles, lifting the kitten from her thighs.

Georgia meows an objection as Mrs. Baxter uses her paw to send me a goodbye wave. I feel silly waving at a cat, but I did it to appease Mrs. Baxter. She exits the vehicle, tosses her oversized purse onto her shoulder, and rests the kitten inside its unzipped top.

"Pretty flowers," she says pointing. "New boyfriend?"

"Definitely not. Here." I extend the flowers to her. "If I keep them, they'll just die."

"Oh, wonderful. I can put them in the center of my dining room table."

She turns on her heels and saunters into the house without so much as a thank you. Perhaps because they were meant for me and I gave them to her, depersonalizing the gift. I chuckle through my nose as I listen to her talk to Georgia through the screen door and climb into my Scion.

I turn the key in the ignition as Mrs. Baxter slams her screen door open and hustles down her stairs. She is holding an old black cordless phone with duct tape around its handle. I roll my window down and she rests her palms on the door as she catches her breath.

"Good lord I'm glad I caught you." She grasps her chest and coughs multiple times before spitting in the bushes next to my driveway. I grimace as she reaches in and grips my shoulder with the hand she used to cover her mouth.

"This is Marcy from down the road on the line. She said that her neighbor has a video of the car that hit Tabitha. Now I think you should go down there and find out who hit your precious baby. Maybe if you can see the license plate, you can report it."

Tabitha did get hit by a car as Mrs. Baxter thought. Perhaps it was just an accident and Tony had nothing to do with it. It all seems so coincidental.

"I don't think I can watch it, Mrs. Baxter."

"I understand. Don't worry. I will head down to Marcy's, and we can watch it together while we drink coffee and gossip."

"That's sweet of you. I have to go now." A tear tugs at the corner of my eye. There is a video. I picture the moment of impact in my head and tears flood my face as I pull away from Mrs. Baxter and take off down the street.

The highway is void of traffic as I travel several miles out of town and pull into a lakeside hotel. I stared at myself in the car mirror for several minutes before getting out. My eyes are red and swollen, and my face aged overnight—too much stress.

The front desk clerk gave me a room with a lake view and a balcony. I take a seat in a resin chair and call Stevie's.

"I'm not coming to work this weekend. Sorry."

Before he asked why, I hung up. I dial the clinic and let them know I won't be in for the rest of the week.

My phone rings as soon as I rest it on the balcony table. It's Mrs. Baxter and I hesitate. Do I really want to know what she saw on that video? The phone stopped ringing and a few seconds later I had a voicemail notification. I take a deep breath and play it back.

'Mia, this is Mrs. Baxter. You will be happy to know I caught the little bastard who hit your Tabitha. Stupid teenage boy down the road. The kid can barely see over the damn windshield of his mother's Chevrolet. He took it without her permission and drove his little brother to the store to buy him candy. Can you believe that? On their way home, Tabitha darted in front of him. He didn't stop because he was afraid he'd get in trouble. Well now he's in a world of shit. I marched right down to his mother's house with a copy of that video. Boy,

did she give him an ass whooping. Well, anyway, I hope you're having a great vacation. Georgia says hi. Bye now.'

A teenager on a joyride with his little brother killed my Tabitha. Not Tony, or Nick or some other sinister stalker. I thought knowing would bring me some sense of closure, but now I feel bad that some kid is getting a walloping by his mother thanks to Mrs. Baxter. It's not his fault, he's just a kid trying to be nice to his little brother. I thought about calling her back and thanking her, but I know she will keep me on the phone forever with gory details I don't need to hear.

The sun glimmers off the water as a tour boat floats a handful of tourists away from the docks. An unknown number calls my phone. I hesitate, then turn it off—no more interruptions. My focus is on myself and nursing this hangover. On the dresser is a menu. After scanning its array of choices, I settled on a grilled chicken salad with iced tea.

I flop onto the king-size bed and think about Tony. He intrigues me in a way I can't explain while, at the same time, scaring the shit out of me. If he is with Nick, why hasn't he taken me back to him? Is this some sick game? Did Nick pay him to torment me and mess with my mind?

The door to my room rattles. When I squint into the peephole, a tray on a rolling cart is all I can see. When I open the door, a young woman greets me.

"Room service," she smiles.

I pass her a five-dollar bill and take the food and tea from her. The mixed green salad steams with grilled chicken on top, and my mouth waters with anticipation. As I take a huge, tasty bite, I moan with pleasure and dance back to the outdoor chair.

Some women in black pants and white dress shirts walk along the waterway carrying a banner and step ladder. They work together to hang the sign high above the walkway. It's advertising the wine festival. I checked the date on my watch. It's this weekend, and I have tickets.

I called the front desk and requested an extension of my stay until Sunday. They told me they usually can't because of the upcoming event, but a wedding party canceled at the last minute, opening my room and a few others. I ask her where I can shop for an outfit, and she gives me two shops that carry my desired attire.

After finishing my lunch, I walked to the closest store the clerk gave me. A mannequin wears a one-shoulder, knee-length toga with a gold embellished belt. It's perfect. The salesperson undresses the display and leads me to the dressing room. When I exit, the woman covers her mouth.

"Wow. That dress is meant for your body." She smiles and points to a mirror behind me.

Hitting above the knee, the outfit made me appear much taller. The salesperson brings over a matching crown and sets it on my head.

"Perfect." The associate claps.

My fizzy locks are a mess, but I see the potential. "Sandals?"

I follow her to a shelf full of gladiator shoes. The woman picks up a pair of glitter white and gold ones. The crisscross straps run to my knees. A little makeup and a fancy side braid with metallic ropes twisted into my hair would complete the outfit. I gave the clerk my credit card and went to the changing room to remove my new clothes.

I've never been so excited to attend an event by myself before. I'm looking forward to a day filled with trying wines and, with any luck, making a few new friends. There are still several days to go, so I fill my schedule with tours, hiking, and swimming in the indoor pool. The abandoned whirlpool entices me with its steaming liquid. I take advantage and drop my tired body into it. Hiking can be a fun and exciting adventure, but if you don't do it often, the result is painful muscles.

A woman enters the room with four children. In my head, I chant, 'Don't come over here,' over and over, but it doesn't work. Her kids plow into the bubbling water all at once, fighting over who gets to lean against the jets. I take a deep breath and try not to lose my cool as one of her boy's stomps on my toe. A sign should say '*no kids allowed*,' but the hotel is family friendly.

I hoist my red, dripping body out of the swirling liquid, grab a towel, and pad my way to the elevators. If I could afford it, I would have paid for the room that included the jacuzzi tub.

The elevator clanks open, and a housekeeper rolls her eyes at the puddle around my feet. She pushes her cart out of the elevator, yanks a cloth from her cart, and tosses it on the ground. I punch the button for my floor, and she sucks her teeth as the metallic partitions clank together.

"Bitch," I murmur as the elevator ascends.

I don't know what she expects. Does she think people are on vacation from their lives so they can clean up after themselves? The whole point of getting away is to leave behind all your responsibilities, including cleaning. I toss my damp towel on the floor, remove my bikini, and climb clothesless into bed. A vacation from my life is what I need, and I'll be damned if I let a snotty housekeeper ruin it for me.

Chapter Ten
Festival

After several exhausting days of sightseeing, I scheduled an appointment at a local spa. Having someone shove their fists into the knots in my muscles isn't my idea of fun. With all the stress I've been dealing with, though, it's called for.

The spa is only a block away. The sun is toasty and ducks behind passing clouds on and off. A slight breeze blows my hair across my face. I opened the business door and saw several women sitting in chairs with cucumber wheels on their eyes. Their heads wear towels, and cotton sticks out from between their toes.

An associate pokes her head around a curtain to greet me. "Mia?"

"Yes."

"Come with me."

The girl takes me down a pale, pink-painted hall lined with images of famous people they have serviced. We turn into a room with soft lighting smelling of flowers. On the table are a robe and towels. The stand next to it has an assortment of oils.

"I'm right outside the door. Give me a shout when I can come back in," the masseuse says.

I peel off my top and bottoms, fold them, and place them in a cubby. The oversized towel is still warm when I cover my naked bottom.

"Ready," I holler to her.

"Wonderful. Let's begin."

The woman's hands spread a sparse amount of hot oil across my back. After an hour of front and back massaging, I finally relax. My muscles are dough, and she made a thin-crust pizza out of me.

She took me into another room after I slipped into the provided robe. A nail specialist showed me a collection of colors. I point to Crimson Fire.

"Excellent choice," the manicurist says.

I join the other ladies once the technician finishes my nails and grab some vegetable slices of my own. My feet sway to the music playing above me. Someone clears their throat beside me, and I turn my head. The cucumber slice on my left eye slides to the floor and rolls away like an unsecured wheel.

"Shit. Sorry," I say to the desk associate.

"Happens all the time."

I checked the time. The festival starts in an hour, and I still need to do my hair and makeup—time to go.

The clouds are almost nonexistent now, and the day is warming up. A group of men in togas walks across the street toward the festival. My legs quicken as I hustle back to my room.

The high-pressure shower pounds my slippery flesh as I scrub excess oil from my body. A shadow catches my eye, startling me.

"Hello? Is someone there?"

No reply. I turn the water off, grab a towel and tiptoe around the corner. The housekeeper is singing and making my bed. The woman jumps at once at the site of my sopping frame staring at her.

"Sorry. I knocked, and when no one answered, I came in." She explains, removing her earbud.

"It's fine. Can I have an extra pillow?"

"No problem," she replies, exiting the room.

When she returns, she rests two pillows on the comforter and drops a couple of mints in a dish by the bed. After she finishes my room, I put on the new outfit and lace up my sandals. My hair is less than cooperative, but it turns out perfect. I swipe my white fabric purse with a metallic zipper and chain strap on my way out the door.

Cars are bumper to bumper trying to enter the parking area. An attendant takes my ticket, punches a hole through the date, and passes me a complimentary glass.

The first wine I tasted was a summer blend. It has blueberries, grapes, and strawberries, and the sticker on the front is a woman in sunglasses and a floppy hat sitting by the ocean. I like the sweetness of it but don't care for the texture, so I move on to the next canopy.

The man behind the display table keeps his hazel eyes on me as he pours more than a sample glass. A woman beside me sticks her empty goblet in his face, and he diverts his attention from me to her. The wine is a semi-sweet red and stimulates every tastebud in my mouth. I toss the remaining liquid into my throat.

"I'd like to buy a bottle," I say to the stocky man as he dribbles a small sample into the customer to my rights glass.

He hands me my purchase but pauses before letting go. "You are a very beautiful woman." His pudgy middle finger lifts away from the bottle and caresses my hand.

Nothing I have ever tried before made me react in such a way, but his behavior has me second-guessing my purchase. I pulled the bottle away from him and handed him cash instead of my credit card. The last thing I need is a second stalker.

The winery is new to the area, and this is their debut flavor. A bare-chested man encapsulates a woman in his arms as she stares up at him on the label. It's seductive, like the wine. I wonder if this is how the man running the tent sees himself. I slide away from his area, and try to avoid turning around, but have no choice due to the crowd. I sense his eyes on my ass right away. Anytime someone stares at me inappropriately, I can always sense it. Even my walking changes as I shift uncomfortably. I skipped several vendors to avoid stopping in his line of sight.

Despite trying many other samples, from multiple other wineries, nothing compares to the one I bought. So, I pop its cork and sit on an empty bench. Before I knew it, half the bottle was gone. My head wobbles a little as I try to focus on the person beside me.

"Hi, Mia."

Tony is wearing a long toga, dark brown sandals, and a crown of gold like mine on his head. His tattoo is clear to me now. Tony's real name is Antonius, and he is hot. Not fire-hot, but the kind of guy who sends a tingle between my thighs hot.

This is the first time I have seen him not in street clothes or having a baseball cap shadowing his face. Tony's chiseled biceps and mysterious demeanor send a wave of curiosity throughout my body.

Tony, however, is not a friend to me or anyone I am familiar with. He is stalking and harassing me with no explanation. Enough is enough.

"No. Stay away from me." I say as I get up and stagger toward the exit.

Tony snatches my upper arm from behind and spins me to face him. I yank myself away, and he puts his hand up. "Let me explain."

"Explain what, Antonius. Did Nick send you? Because I am not going back. No matter what he says or what tricks he tries to pull, I am done with that life. I need to feel safe and have control," I argue, crossing my arms.

"No, Mia. Nick didn't send me."

He said his name as if he knew Nick but didn't elaborate.

"Let me take you to dinner so we can talk."

"Dinner? Are you crazy or something?" I say as I squint and toss my hands in front of me.

"No, I just thought…"

"Thought, what? Just because you kept me from driving drunk and beating up a guy, we are suddenly going out?"

"Maybe," Tony says with a crooked smile.

I couldn't help myself. There is something about the way he looks at me that makes it hard to stay mad at him. I want to scream and yell at him but can't seem to bring myself to do it.

"You're nuts," I chuckle.

There is a long, awkward pause between us as we both relax. It was short-lived as I remember what Tony said.

"I know you said Nick didn't send you, but the way you said his name has me wondering if you know him."

Tony focuses on a dirty paper plate on the ground in between us. He shifts it to the side with his sandal and takes a step closer.

"Yes."

"Yes, as in you know him because of who he is, or yes because you know him personally."

"Personally."

"That's freaking super. Stay away from me."

"Mia, listen."

"No, Tony, you listen. I'm stressed, anxious, and, most of all, tired. So, whatever you are doing here, it's over. Tell Nick or whoever hired you to harass me that I have had it with these games. The next person who fucks with me, I am shooting in the face."

"Mia, you don't have or own a gun." Tony grins.

"Yeah, well, I am buying one right now, dammit," I scoff and stalk away like a child.

He doesn't follow. I jog across the street in front of traffic, and multiple horns beep at me. My middle finger flies high at them as I step onto the curb and launch the hotel lobby door open. The elevator couldn't ascend fast enough as I pounded the button for my floor. Dizziness makes walking in a straight line difficult as the doors clank open, and I stagger down the hall.

When I turn the corner, my breath catches in my lungs. Tony is leaning on the wall next to my door, holding the bottle I left behind.

Chapter Eleven
Turning Point

"Go away, Tony."

"And let this bottle of wine go to waste? I think not." Tony says without smiling.

I shove passed him into my room and try shutting the door. His foot wedges in between, and I push against it. He leans inward and enters the room.

"Please, go," I bawl, finally losing my shit.

"Mia, stop fighting this."

"Fighting what? I don't know what this is." I wipe frustrated tears from my eyes. "Why can't everyone leave me alone?"

All the flyers and brochures on the kitchen counter float onto the floor as I swipe them off it.

The phone next to the bed rings. Tony crosses the room and answers it.

"Everything is fine. Thanks," he says, hanging up. "The front desk received a noise complaint."

My butt sinks into the mattress as emotions overwhelm me, and I sob uncontrollably. Tony stoops before me.

"Don't cry, Mia."

"Please, tell me why this is all happening."

"Mia, look at me."

My head turns, and I watch the clouds in the sky float past the window. Tony takes my chin and moves it back to face him. Our eyes lock, and he narrows the gap between us.

"I'm sorry for everything. Never in a million years did I expect this to happen."

"What?" I whisper.

"Us."

He kisses me, making my head prickle. I touch my lips with my fingertips as I stand up and place my palms on the granite kitchen island.

"Please, tell me who you are," I plead as I turn and face him.

"All you need to know is what started as a job has become much more."

"What do you mean job? More how?" I ask as I cross my arms. "Who do you work for?"

"Something about you makes my heart beat faster. When I close my eyes, you visit me in my dreams," Tony says as he strolls toward me. "I want you, Mia. I need you."

I dropped my limbs and moved away from him. There is something between us. I can feel it too, but I am afraid to react. He's not a nice person, but my body is saying one thing and my mind another. What if this is a trap set by Nick? If I give in to my desire, and this is part of some elaborate scheme, I'm dead. Everything that has happened thus far has led us to this moment—this decision. If I do this, there is no going back. I can't. It's not right.

"I need you to leave."

He's coming closer. I can feel him behind me.

"Nick will kill us both if he finds you here," I weep.

His breath shifts the hair on my neck as he nearly touches me.

"He's going to kill me."

Tony wraps his arms around me from behind and kisses my neck. His touch sends a wave of pleasure straight between my legs. My breaths quicken, and he senses my lust.

"Let him try," Tony murmurs as he raises my toga. "Say yes, Mia."

"Tony...I..." His thumbs hook the fabric of my underwear and pause, waiting for permission.

His mouth hovers by my ear as he whispers, "I want to be inside you."

The tingle on my lower lips becomes so intense, I want to touch them myself. As if he senses my desire for him, he entices me further. "Let me taste your juices."

My breathing accelerates, and my whole body tingles at the mere mention of him wanting to taste me, tossing any guilt I have out the window. Alcohol may have played a role in my decision. At least, that is what I plan on telling myself when this is all over.

"Fuck me," I murmur, arching my back toward him.

He rips my lace panties to the floor and shoves his face into my backside. I thought I might blow a gasket right then, but I forced myself to think of something else. Kissing one cheek, then the other, he stands and stuffs his stallion-sized cock into me. Tony's callused hand cups over my mouth, stifling my screams, as he thrusts into me.

Fluids burst from the depths of my soul as he spins me and sets me on the countertop. I wrap my fingers in his hair and force his head further between my legs as he laps up my liquid pleasure like a thirsty dog. Tony sucks the life out of my lower lips and nibbles my inner thigh.

This is wrong. So wrong. All of it. But since I left Nick, I haven't been with anyone else. I must be crazy, for I am having the best sex of my life with my stalker, who may work for Nick. But I don't care for my loins long for attention, and this man is giving me all of it and then some.

My crisis of consciousness is short-lived as he takes my breasts into his mouth, sucking my nipples hard. He lifts my body off the counter and carries me to bed. His fingers intertwine with mine as he grinds into me slowly.

"Harder," I whisper.

He picks up the pace, but it's not good enough. I want it all.

"Hurt me. I want it harder. Now give it to me," I order.

Tony rams into me. My nails dig into his spine with every painful thrust. I pull him into me so deep I feel him in my stomach. I've never wanted someone so bad in my life. If this is our one and only time, I want it to be worth it. Every damn minute of it.

"Turn me over and take me from behind."

"With pleasure."

He flips me over, bends my arms behind my back, holds my wrists with one hand, and takes my neck with the other. Pushing his length into me harshly from behind, I cry out as he thrusts into me over and over. The frame beneath us cracks and breaks, but he doesn't stop. I clench the hotel pillow between my teeth and try not to scream as I orgasm. Tony moans as he slams his load inside me.

"Wow," Tony pants as he falls beside me.

I can't breathe or move. I lie face down, suffocating myself with a blanket. Tony rolls me onto my side and holds me around my waist. I push his hand off, stagger to my feet and scramble for my clothing.

"This is a mistake. Nick is going to kill me."

Tony stretches across the length of the bed with a broad satisfied smile and stares at my frantic state.

"I won't let him."

"That's sweet, but he's dangerous. No one can keep me safe from him. Now, please leave," I huff.

Tony slides to the end of the bed, seizes my thighs, and draws me to him.

"I'm leaving, but I'm coming back."

Tony stands up and steps around me. His eyes scan the room and stop at his boxers. After pulling them on, he pecks me on the forehead and heads for the door.

"Tony. Tell me who you are."

His hand pauses on the handle, and his eyes meet mine. "Someday. But not today."

When he continues through the door, I chuck my wine at the wall, shattering it. The red liquid travels like rain down a windowpane and pools on the floor. What have I done? If this is a test, I just failed.

The fermented grape puddle moves toward an expensive-looking area rug. If it stains it, they may charge me. I use a towel to sop it up and a wet washcloth to cleanse the staining plaster.

The spot where the bottle struck the wall left a smooth semi-circular dent. It isn't noticeable from a distance, so I call it a win. Here I worry about a stained rug when we broke the bed. I will need to rig it up somehow and hopefully it can stay together until the next person sleeps in it. Won't they be surprised when it collapses to the floor?

Warm juices slide down my inner thigh. "Gross," I whisper to the empty room.

The phone blares once more, making me jump. If I owned it, it would be in the garbage by now. Another grievance, I'm sure. I ignored it and headed to the bathroom.

The steaming hot shower doesn't change my feelings. Guilt can be a fickle bastard. It takes me to the floor of the tub.

I cry until the remaining liquid comes from above me instead of inside. My skin coats itself with goosebumps as the water turns cold. The silver drain swirls my grime and shame into the sewer and disappears.

A feeling of dread overwhelms me, and every part of me shakes. I haven't felt this scared since I left Nick.

Tony was a mistake. Plain and simple. The next time I see him, I'm telling him that whatever this may be, is over. There is nothing more to say until he explains who he is. I'm not some toy he can play with.

Anger gives me the strength to stand and shut the water off with a tremoring hand. The mirror is foggy, so I wipe it with my palm and gaze at my reflection. Mascara darkens the underside of my eyes, and I dab it with a dry washcloth. From now on, I am running the show—no more games. I am in control of my destiny. This is my life. No more nonsense. Nothing can stop me now.

I wrap myself in a towel, throw the door aside, and walk right into Nick's chest.

Chapter Twelve
Fear

Nick gazes down at his now damp shirt. I take a step away from him and raise my hands in surrender. His soldier boys stand behind him and remain silent as he unbuttons it and throws it on the comforter.

Nick's broad, muscular sternum is hairier than I remember. He stares at the decorative tiles on the ceiling and lets out an exaggerated breath.

"Gentlemen, please wait in the hall. Mia and I have some things to discuss in private."

All three of them put their heads down and exited without a word. Nick seizes my arms and tosses me onto the bed when the door clicks. The towel covering me yanks from my grasp, as he snatches it and chucks it on the floor. He grabs my face and squeezes it hard when I open my mouth to speak.

"No one leaves me, Mia. No one. Do you have any idea how exposed I am? The FBI is breathing down my neck, and other families are moving in on our territory, and you've got me chasing you across the state."

"Nick, I'm sorry."

"Sorry? You snuck off in the middle of the night without a word. No note, no trace, nothing, and all you can say to me is sorry. Do you have any idea what you have put me through and the pain you have caused? Why, Mia?"

"Because I was afraid."

"Afraid? I've never touched you in any way. I gave you anything you ever wanted, and you left because you're scared?" He shouts in my face as he lifts me upright. "Get dressed. We are leaving."

I bite my tongue when he throws me backward, and metallic liquid fills my palate. My fingernails fold over as I pinch the white pillow, grit my teeth, and proclaim, "I'm not going anywhere."

Trying to take my own advice and be in control of my life earns me a slap across the face. I try and collect myself, but Nick doesn't allow me the opportunity. Stars dance before my eyes as my body sails through the air and lands on the area rug.

Nick takes my hair in his grasp and whispers in my ear. "Now you have a reason to be afraid. Go put on some clothes."

He releases me and drops my suitcase on the laminate at the edge of the carpet beside my knees. I unzip it and take out sweatpants and a T-shirt. Nick snatches them away and stuffs them in the wastebasket.

"Wear something sexy. We're stopping for dinner," he proclaims as he punches a number into his phone.

The only dress I have with me is a rose sundress with little white daisies on it. This isn't what he wants, and he is disappointed. I flinch when Nick crouches in front of me. He removes lace underwear and bra from the pile and puts them in my hand.

"The summer dress is acceptable for now. We can stop and buy something nicer. Okay?" Nick says, stroking my shoulder with his thumb.

I nod. He lifts me to my feet, takes my panties, and stoops down. I lift my limbs, one at a time, and he hikes them up to my waist. His eyes don't leave mine as he slips my arms into my bra and fastens it. Once he helps me into my dress, he calls his men back into the room.

One of them hands him a clean black button-up dress shirt. Nick buttons it, keeping his attention on me the entire time. Air staggers out in intermittent huffs from his mouth as though he wants to charge and hurt me more but doesn't. Nick is restraining his temper, something he doesn't often do.

"Grab her things. All of them." Nick orders.

His men pick up my luggage and clear out the toiletries from the bathroom. Nick takes me by the elbow and leads me down the elevator, through the lobby, and into a black SUV. I peer around outside, searching for Tony, but don't see him.

The silence is unnerving as he sits beside me and stares out the window. Rage emanates from him like heat from a stove, making me draw my arms against myself. I'm waiting for him to snap like I have seen him do before to others who have crossed him.

Tony's semen moistens my underwear, and I shift in my seat as Nick places his hand on my knee.

"I reacted poorly, Mia. I'm sorry."

"Nick, why me? Tons of girls throw themselves at you every day."

"I want and love you, not them, Mia. Don't you get it? Once something is mine, it is always mine."

A singular tear rolls down my face. It's all I have left in me. The rest washed down the drain along with the remnants of my life. The SUV stops in front of a shop in town. In the window, a short, crimson cocktail dress with spaghetti straps hangs from a display. Nick gazed at it as he held the door for me. He's always loved red.

The man working pulls the attire from the hanger and gives it to me. I draw the curtain in the changing room aside, but before I close it, Nick steps inside. He sits on the bench in the confined space and interlaces his fingers on his lap.

"I missed you, Mia. So much has happened."

My lack of response irritates him, but I don't care. He hurt me, and now I'm making him suffer. The silky fabric slips over my near-naked skin like melting butter. I turn to the mirror, and he slips his palms up the inner thigh of my left leg. My legs clamp shut, and he forces them back open.

"Don't fight me, Mia."

"Boss?" One of his men hollers from behind the divide.

"What?" Nick shouts as he slides his palms from my trembling frame.

"Sorry, sir. Your father is on the line."

No one, except his father, could have stopped him from touching me in the dressing room. When he calls, Nick always answers.

I grabbed my sundress and sandals and reentered the sales floor. Nick points to heels on a rack on his way outdoors to take his call. Of course, he chooses a red pair. The salesman finds my size and rests them by my feet.

"Is everything okay?" The associate asks a little too loud.

"She's fine. Do your job." One of Nick's men warns him.

Nick's outside waving his hands as he hollers into his cell. He pauses when he catches me watching him and turns away. The clerk brings out the dress and shoes. One of the guys passes him a handful of too much cash—hush money.

Nick enters the shop, wraps his arm around me, and leans in. "Mmmm. You look good enough to eat."

Inside my head, I laugh. Someone already ate me earlier. If he knew, I would be dead by now. Nick either doesn't know Tony or doesn't want to ask me about him. For now, I am keeping my thoughts to myself.

Something about Nick is different. His eyes have a sadness to them that I have never seen before. Perhaps leaving him hurt more than I thought it would—the side of my face aches. I rub it with my palm, and Nick takes my hand away. He interlocks his fingers with mine, and I flinch when he kisses the back of my hand.

Nick tightens his grip, crushing my appendages in his grasp when I try and pull away.

"Don't," he warns as he leads me in the direction of his idling vehicle.

He may have found me, but he can't have me. I escaped his clutches once, and I plan to do it again.

Chapter Thirteen
Dinner with the Devil

After driving for almost an hour, we arrived at an Italian restaurant of Nick's choosing. The hostess seats us by a picture window overlooking the city. We have a table for twelve, even though we are a party of five. His men sit at the far end.

The waitress drops a menu before me, and Nick removes it. I opened my mouth to object and thought better of it. He reviews the options and settles on a filet for himself and a salad for me. I love steak as much as an addict loves drugs, and he knows this. This is part of my punishment.

The server returns moments after taking our order with a bottle of champagne. Nick slides his glass down to her, and she fills it halfway. I lift mine, and Nick rests his hand on the rim—none for me.

After she walks away, I stand and toss my napkin onto the tablecloth. Nick's men do the same, but Nick doesn't move. "Sit down, Mia."

"Why are you doing this to me?"

"Sit down, now." He insists with darkening eyes.

I flop back into my seat, place my hands in front of me, and flick my fingernails. Nick's hand encapsulates my fingers, and he issues a stern order. "Stop it."

A basket of bread arrives, but I don't bother reaching for it. Nick takes a warm slice, spreads a pat of butter on it, and sets it before me.

"Thanks," I say, accepting his offer.

Trying to control things and take what I want is getting me nowhere. So, I play along.

"Nick, may I have some water?"

"The water is free," he says, handing it to me.

After gulping the entire glass, I set it down and took an enormous bite of bread. Nick's brow furrows as he prepares to address my antics. A waiter appears at the head of the table with our dinner. I peer behind him, looking for our waitress, but she doesn't appear.

The man sets a filet before me, and Nick shoots him an evil glance. Another one comes off the tray and is set in front of Nick. No salad.

His men stand and stare at this exchange. They all have pasta, so this is not a mix-up. Each one moves their blazers aside and places their hands on their weapons.

"What the fuck is this?" Nick points at the mignon sitting in front of me. "I ordered her a salad."

"Sir, someone gave the kitchen a message changing the order," the waiter insists.

"Well, I did not do it. She got a pile of greens, and I got steak. Not two steaks, one. That's what I asked for, and that's what I want."

"Nick, it's fine. There is no sense wasting it now," I say, reaching for a knife.

Nick's fist pounds onto the table. "It won't go to waste, Mia."

He stabs the meat before me with his fork and drops it on his plate. I stare, mouth gaped open at his selfish display of power. My fingers curl around the blade still in my grasp. One of his guys leans over me and crushes my hand in his until I let go of the weapon while the waiter sneaks away.

The waitress returns with what Nick ordered for me moments later, but I've lost my appetite. My utensil moves the food around but never reaches my mouth. His men all relax, sit down and dive into their pasta dishes—sauce splatters about as they swirl it on their spoons and stuff it in their oversized faces—my nose wrinkles in disgust.

I remain silent as Nick devours two steaks like an animal that just awakened from a long winter slumber. With every stab of his fork, buttery garlic wine sauce splatters on the white tablecloth. His knife scrapes across his plate like nails on a chalkboard, sending chills down my back. I rub my arms to comfort myself, but it isn't working. With each bite, he takes a moment to glare at me as he chews his meat. The wheels inside his head turn, debate, and plan my future every time he swallows.

Across the room, the waitress watches us as she exchanges words with the waiter. She scans the room and says one last thing before stalking out of site. The water is doing its job, and I stand to use the restroom. If the waitress went into the bathroom, I could ask to see the note the kitchen received.

"Where are you going?" Nick asks.

"Restroom."

He nods to one of his men to go with me. I grimace and storm away from the table.

The hallway to the restroom is a Tuscan sunset color. The hanging paintings are of Italian villages framed in gold. I stop and admire one next to the emergency exit. As if Nick's crony reads my mind, he blocks my escape and pushes the ladies' room door open.

I roll my eyes and duck inside. There are two stalls, and I picked the larger one. Nothing is worse than sitting down and having my knees touch the door. The stall beside me is empty when I peek under, looking for feet. I cover the seat with paper and release my bladder dam of pressure. When I wipe, more of Tony's bodily goop falls out of me.

I slap my forehead at my stupidity as I realize how Nick found me—the credit card. He knows my password. It is the same for everything, so I don't forget. He told me before I should change it as it is not secure, but I didn't listen. All he would need to do is have some female call and give all my information to see where I used the card last. I've been so careful to use cash, except for that one time. What a stupid mistake. One I hope to never make again.

As for Tony, I am not sure how he found me. Perhaps he followed me when I bolted from my house. I do a few more passes, removing more juices from my private space, and flush.

Someone changed the order, and if Nick didn't do it, then who? Messing with Nick is like playing Russian roulette. His response is unpredictable.

The mirror before me reveals a new bruise joining the one from Joan. Nick never asked me what happened.

The door cracks and Nick's guy peeks inside. "Wrap it up, Mia. My food is getting cold."

I shake the moisture from my palms and bump past him. Nick wipes his face with a napkin when I sit down. He raises his hand to the waitress, and she carries the check over. My meal is gone, and so is his patience.

He tosses three hundred-dollar bills on the table, seizes my hand, and leads me outside. The SUV door is ajar and ready for us. Nick whispers to his driver, who steps out.

He grips my neck and brings my face almost against his. "Mia don't ever embarrass me again. Understand?"

I nod, and he kisses me hard on the mouth, splitting my lip. Nick smears it with his thumb and knocks on the tinted glass. His men load into the vehicle and exchange glances when they see the beard-like smudge of blood on my mouth and chin. Nick licks his finger and removes the distraction.

He pulls my body close and forces my head onto his shoulder as we pull away from the curb. "Shut your eyes, beautiful. We have a long drive ahead of us."

Chapter Fourteen
Lost in the Dark

The view is pitch black. The GPS is leading us through the backwoods of Upstate NY, and now we are on a hill.

Reception comes and goes as the guys try to read a paper map from the glovebox. A buck, with a massive rack, freezes on the roadway. Our driver slams on the brakes to avoid striking him.

"Stupid animals," Nick hisses in frustration as he snatches the map and turns on the light above him. "Here. This is where we are. At the next fork, go right, and it should take us down."

His driver makes a sharp turn and almost hits a herd of deer. Dozens of them meander before the bumper, oblivious of their danger.

Fog envelops the SUV as we round another corner and navigate multiple winding roads. The thick white curtain in front of us limits visibility to only a few feet.

A loud bang, followed by a sudden wheel jerk, throws me into Nick. The driver eases the vehicle into a grassy area beside a trench.

"Stay in the car," Nick insists as he steps out with his men.

Muffling voices bicker for a few minutes, then fall silent. Nick opens the door and slides in.

"Tire is flat. The guys are putting on the spare." Nick says as he stares at my naked legs. "Come sit on me."

"Nick, I'm tired."

"Mia, stop making me ask twice," Nick orders, smacking his pants' surface.

I remove my heels and straddle his body as instructed.

"Kiss me," he demands.

I bend down, peck his cheek, and wipe it off.

Nick laughs through his nose as he purses his lips. "What's the problem, Mia?"

"I'm exhausted," I lie as I try to move away.

Nick slips his hands high under my dress and grabs my thighs with an uncomfortable force. "Yeah, well, I'm not. Now, take off those undies."

My eye twitches, and my temples throb. I don't want him inside me or touching me.

His fingers wrap around my lace panties and pull.

"No," I say in a firm, clear voice. "No means no."

I shy away from his shocked face, lift my leg off his, and rotate away.

Nick seizes my knee hard, mid-way off him, and screams. "What the hell is this?" His eyes are staring between my legs.

Nick yanks my limbs apart and uses his thumb to swipe an oval, purple discoloration high on my inner thigh. "Mia, is that a hickey?"

My body trembles in his grasp as I recall Tony being down there earlier in the day. He nibbled and sucked on me in many locations, but I didn't think to check myself for marks.

Nick seizes my underwear, rips them away, and inhales their scent.

His face darkens, and an eerie silence comes over him right before he yells. "Whore!"

The door whips open, and Nick flies out, screaming at the night sky. I lean against the opposing exit, frozen in place, shaking. His men ask him what happened, but Nick doesn't reply. He glares inside the SUV at my folded body.

Without warning, he reaches in, grabs both of my ankles, and yanks me out of the vehicle. I reach frantically for the door framework to keep him from taking me. My back smacks hard on the asphalt as I bounce onto the ground.

"Boss, what is going on?" One of his guys asks.

They know his father frowns upon violence against women unless they break a rule. Under the circumstances, I think his father would make an exception.

Nick doesn't do well with betrayal. We are not together, in my opinion, but in his twisted mind, he considers this cheating.

"Who is he, Mia?"

"Nick, please. I'm sorry."

"There's that fucking word again. Sorry. Well, I'm sorry too."

Nick picks me up by my hair and drags me like a caveman into the woods. His men stay behind, unsure of what to do.

Branches and debris dig into my flesh as he weaves through the dense forest landscape. I thrash about, digging my nails into his hand. Red liquid drains from the holes I create and travels down my wrist.

"Tell me who he is, Mia. I want his name."

"His name is Tony. Now, please, let me go."

He pauses in between two enormous pines. I thought he would release me, but he wrapped his hand tighter around my hair. Now he's yanking and pulling me at the same time. The further into the brush we went, the darker everything became.

The moon supplies a small amount of light and is visible in sparse amounts through the canopy. Nick tosses me on the ground in a well-lit clearing and removes his belt. I crawl away but not fast enough to avoid the lashing. Repeated strikes sting my uncovered backside as he whips me over and over while I cry for forgiveness.

"What's his last name?"

"I don't know, Nick. Please, stop."

He climbs on top of me, seizes me by the shoulders, and shakes me like a rattle. "I wanted to have a family and grow old together."

The ringing in my ears starts quiet and grows louder as he thrashes my head about.

"We still can, baby," I offer, stroking his chest.

"You ruined everything."

Tears travel down his face as his heart breaks, and so does mine. I didn't realize the impact leaving him would have. He takes my hand away from his heart, kisses it, and sets it down.

Nick rubs the silky fabric over my breasts, grips the neckline, and rips the dress almost in half. I flop under him as he takes my throat in his hands and squeezes.

The vessels in my right eye pop with a sharp, stabbing burst as I scratch his arms and kick my legs. Black spots form in my line of vision, and the lights of death wrap around me.

I pray to God to help me as I lose the strength to fight him.

A single gunshot echoes through the trees, stopping Nick, silencing his cries, and saving my life.

Chapter Fifteen
Prey

Nick loosens his grasp without letting go. Shouting comes from the road, and Nick climbs off me.

A 9 mm appears from inside his jacket as he tries to lift me. My legs fail, and I fall back to the grass.

"Move your ass," he screams while keeping his focus on the trees.

The lack of oxygen weakened me, and I couldn't stop him from dragging me through the brush. Sticks dig into my uncovered feet as I fumble along the downed branches Nick is yanking me over.

The closer we came to the road, the more my stomach twisted. Something is wrong. There is no more noise, not from the forest, the road, or Nick's men. No one is around when we breach the tree line.

Nick puts me and his gun in front of him as we round the SUV. His guys, all of them, are in the ditch. Blood drips from a bullet hole in one man's forehead. The other has a gaping wound across his throat. The last one's head is backward like an entity took over his body and rotated it, and I am silent—a tiny smile tugs at the corner of my mouth. Nick is unprotected.

"Mother fucker," Nick hisses as he shoves me into the back seat and wedges himself behind the wheel. The former driver was only five feet three inches. A dwarf compared to Nick's six-foot-one frame. The SUV hops into motion as Nick slams on the gas, traveling too fast down the hill.

"Nick, slow down, or you'll kill us both."

"You're already dead to me," he glares at my reflection.

He still plans to kill me. I need to decide my own fate rather than let him choose it for me. A car whips behind us with its high beams distracting him. I reach in front, grab his throat, and crush his Adam's apple in my grasp. Nick holds on for dear life as he struggles to drive and free himself from my grip. The vehicle squeals around the corner and loses control.

A vast oak tree stops everything. It ceases time, the vehicle, and me.

The force of the crash launches me in between the driver and passenger seats. Blood fills my mouth, and pain covers every inch of me.

Glass shatters next to Nick's head, and a gun barrel enters. A person wearing all black, with his face concealed, rests a silencer against Nick's temple.

"Who the fuck are you?" Nick slurs from behind the airbag.

The shadowy figure says nothing as he squeezes the trigger—warm brain tissue splatters across my face. I cry out. "Please, don't hurt me."

A flash of light from a camera blinds me. The man vanishes from sight, and I wet my pants. Footsteps crunch on gravel around to my side of the vehicle, but I can't move. I fight to keep my bowels from evacuating my body.

Part of me is broken, and the rest is shaking—a ringing phone lands on my abdomen, and a woman answers.

"9-1-1, what's your emergency?"

Tears burst from my eyes. He's not going to kill me.

"Hello? This is an emergency line. The police are on their way."

My strength is draining away from me, and I'm dizzy. Goosebumps cover the entire surface of my skin. I'm cold or dying. Perhaps both.

The figure vanishes as I muster up the energy to mutter a single word. "Help."

"Ma'am, are you injured?"

"Yes...I...."

"Okay. I'm dispatching an ambulance. Stay with me. The police are a few minutes out."

The dispatcher continues to speak, but I can't. So, I listen to her calming voice. Blue and red colors flash through the shattered windshield, lighting up the dark forest. Within seconds, a flashlight shines into the slits of my eyes. A uniformed man reaches into the smashed window, removing the phone.

"Don't move."

Another officer puts his hand through the driver's side and presses his fingertips to Nick's neck.

"He's dead. I'll call the coroner."

Duh. If you peer through the circle in his head, you can see me on the other side. The air is thick and hard to breathe. I cough, and stabbing discomfort shoots throughout my ribcage as I weep. Sirens become louder as they approach.

The officer squeezed my hand. "Hang on. The ambulance is here."

Paramedics rush to my side but can't open the door. Firefighters step in and use prying tools. The grinding, metal-on-metal, is deafening as the door breaks off.

"Ma'am, where does it hurt?" the paramedic asks, raising my eyelids.

"Ribs. Can't breathe."

"They're fractured, and one is coming through the skin. Hold still. I'm injecting something for pain, so we can move you. It's still going to hurt like hell, but it will help some. All right? What happened to your dress?"

I can't answer. Within seconds of administering the shot, my head is wobbling, and I can't focus. A stretcher crashes into position, and a man, dressed in firefighter gear reaches inside the vehicle. He picked me up with care, but it didn't matter. Torturous burning travels through my chest and body as I scream.

The tips of my fingers are blue, and my head darts from one face to the next as I panic.

"Ma'am, remain calm."

Calm? Would he be calm if brain matter covered his face, and one of his ribs were protruding through his body?

My head falls to the side as the gurney bumps across the road heading to the waiting transport.

Right before they loaded me into the back, I saw him. In the trees, high above the ground, the man in black is watching.

I point, but the paramedic isn't paying attention as the wheeled bed slides inside and the doors slam. A hand smacks the back, and we roll away with lights and sirens screaming.

The paramedic's hand is beside me, and I squeeze it in a pattern. Three quick grips followed by three long ones and three faster ones.

He brings his face close to mine and says, "Help is already here."

I shake my head with furrowed brows, and he turns his ear to my lips.

"He's watching us," I whisper.

"Who?"

I don't know who, so I have no response for him. Instead, I stay silent and focus on the peach, fleshy matter stuck to the remnants of my dress. The paramedic grabs a disinfecting wipe and cleans the material of bodily tissue. He reaches for my face, and I recoil away from his touch. He pauses and throws the used wipe in the trash without touching me.

"They hurt you, didn't they?"

I nod, and my mouth turns downward in a deep frown.

"I'm sorry this happened to you, but I'm glad they're dead. Anyone who hurts a woman in such a manner shouldn't be allowed to live. No, means no. Any man who doesn't take that to heart deserves punishment. Don't tell anyone I said that, or they'll fire me for sure."

He gazes toward the front where the driver focuses on the road.

When he turns his attention back to me, he takes my hand and squeezes it softly. "You may have some scars from this fight, but you survived it. Time heals all wounds, but it doesn't mean there won't be any proof of what you went through. Let it be a reminder of your strength to carry on and keep living. You are a strong, beautiful woman. Someday, you will be happy, and this will be nothing but a memory. Until then, focus on getting better and stronger so you can live to fight another day."

Snot shoots from my nose and brings blood with it. The paramedic wipes it away and leans toward the driver.

"How close are we?"

"Five minutes," the driver announces.

"Almost there," he says, squeezing my hand as my eyes become too heavy to hold open. "Hang in there. You're going to be okay."

Chapter Sixteen
Nothing to Say

The medical facility's air is cold and reeks of disinfectant when I wake up. Everything hurts. My heart, body, and soul suffer a devastating blow.

Nick tried to kill me, but I didn't wish him dead. His gruesome death may haunt me for life, and I wonder if this place offers counseling or therapy.

The bed is uncomfortable. The hospital does this to keep people from wanting to stay forever. I would. A comfortable place to rest, on-site healthcare, bathroom, room service, and cable. Who would want anything more? Not here, however. My room doesn't have a television or any form of entertainment.

Voices echo beyond the door to my room. I reach with my right hand and fumble for the guardrail. Once I have it, I grip the metal and roll myself onto my back. If my ribs didn't already have a fracture, I would have thought I may have broken them again. A kick to the face would have been more pleasurable.

The motion next to me catches me off guard. An unfamiliar man in a navy-blue suit sits in a leather accent chair under the window. His slicked-back gray hair does little to hide the bald spot on top. In his hand, he taps a notepad with a pen.

"Miss Galano, I'm Agent Corbin with the FBI." The legs of his seat scrape across the floor as he inches closer to me. "I need to ask you some questions."

"No."

"Well, I have to ask," he smiles and rests the tip of his pen on the paper. "You've been unconscious for a couple of days."

I grimace and press the call button. "Ask away, but I'm not interested in giving a statement."

The nurse creeps in and checks my IV bag. "Having pain?"

"Yes." I swallow hard and furrow my brows. "Tell him to leave, please."

"It's not up to me. Sorry." The woman pats my shoulder, injects medicine in my lines, and pours some ice water before exiting.

The medication burns through my veins, and I soar around the room like Mary Poppins a few minutes later. If only I owned her magic umbrella. I would hit this moron with it and fly out of this miserable place.

"Mia, who shot Nick?"

"I don't know. The person wore a mask."

"Describe him. Height, weight estimate, White, Black, Hispanic?"

"The man dressed all in black and covered his face and skin. Now, please leave."

Tears run down my face and ears as my eyes grow heavy. The medication tires me making words mumble from my failing lips.

"What, Mia?"

"A shadow killed Nick," I murmur.

"What?" the agent asks, leaning his ear almost against my mouth. "What's his name?"

"Shadow," I slur and grin before passing out.

My life is as empty as my room is now. Someone wanted Nick dead. If I'm being honest, many people did.

To ignore the obvious would be foolish. The masked man could be Tony. But why? He never told me why he followed me, how he knew Nick, or why he threw my life into chaos. Tony is the only person who can answer my questions, but he's not here. Perhaps he lied about knowing Nick. Anyone with a computer can find articles and arrest records for him. So, what's Tony's role in all this?

A nurse's aide shuffles through the door, carrying a bouquet of red roses. She places them beside me and sniffs their blooms.

"Here's the card." The nurse hands me the envelope and walks away.

Inside, written in Tony's distinctive handwriting, is a short message.

I'm sorry.
Tony

The image on the front is a Pug puppy with a depressed face. The phrase underneath says, 'Sorry you're sad.'

Sad? Try mad. I put the irrelevant note back in its holder and tucked it under my buttocks.

"Those are beautiful flowers," Agent Corbin says, standing in the doorway with a file in his grasp. "Who are they from?"

I shrug my shoulders and avert my eyes.

"Here are some pictures for you to review."

"I said the person's face was covered."

The agent opens the folder on my abdomen. The first picture is of Nick's dead face with a white sheet covering him to his collarbone. My mouth drops open, and I side-swipe the images away from me.

My hands shake as I remember the moment Nick died. His eyes were empty of life, and the opening in his head was dripping blood onto my arm and his console.

"My apologies, Mia. I thought they removed the autopsy pictures." The agent scoops the pile off the floor and sorts out the upsetting ones. "Let's start over."

Agent Corbin is lying to me. The image of Nick with a giant hole in his head is meant to intimidate and scare me into helping. I'm not an idiot, but he thinks I am.

"All I want is some information. Anything, relevant or not, is helpful."

Agent Corbin rests them one at a time on my abdomen. One after another of Nick's enemies, former lovers, and friends. No, Tony. Not a single mention of him. Perhaps he's not involved at all.

One of the headshots is an older image of Nick's father, Carmine. Few people have met him in person, as no one below Nick can access him. I never had a chance to meet him. Nick kept our relationship close to the vest. I have seen old pictures of him. One of which the agent has. He reminds me of Nick. I think I told him that the first time he showed me a photo of his father and mother. It was on their wedding day. His mother is so beautiful. Her dress would make Hollywood stars jealous. I'm glad I never had the chance to meet them. It would have made leaving harder. Only Carmine's closest friends and family can be in the same room as him and have his address. He's a powerful man with powerful enemies. Nick planned to have us meet a week after I left to announce our engagement. He never gave me the ring. His proposal was as rushed as my answer—a spur-of-the-moment decision after a wild night of sex.

"Sorry. I have nothing to say."

Agent Corbin turns his back to me and wipes his face. His cheeks inflate as he lets out a frustrated breath. The stress line between his eyes is more noticeable when he faces me.

"Mia, do you have any idea the danger you're in? Nick and his men are dead. You're a witness and the only person who may be able to help find his killer. I need to know everything, relevant or not."

"I'm sorry, Mr. Corbin. I have nothing to say."

The agent snatches the folder and storms out of the room. I gaze at the cloudy sky through my window. Lightning staggers to the ground in a jagged slow descent, illuminating the hills.

In a few days, when the hospital discharges me, I'm driving home, packing my bags, and leaving. As much as I love my house, I'm not safe there anymore.

Chapter Seventeen
Random

Have you ever wished your life could be different? Who pulls the strings of fate anyways?

I believe our paths are chosen for us from the moment we are born. The result is the same, no matter how often you try to change things.

Leaving Nick is the scariest decision I've made in my entire life. How did it help me? What changed? I ran away from him and started over, but he still found me. To make matters worse, I transformed him in some way. Nick never touched me before, but something happened after I left.

Stopping his medications would explain all his behavior. Borderline personality disorder caused Nick to have violent outbursts and terrible mood swings in his younger years. He took his pills on schedule when we dated. The prescriptions didn't take away all the symptoms—more like they took the edge off.

Perhaps this is my fault. I broke him, and he stopped caring.

Fool. There is no way someone like me could break a man like Nick. His father would never allow it—his father. I imagine he received word of his son's gruesome death.

Agent Corbin said I was in danger. I wonder if he thinks Carmine is coming for me.

"Mia? Earth to Mia," a woman says, interrupting my thoughts.

"Sorry. What?"

"I'm taking you down to X-ray so we can take another chest image."

"Shit. How bad is it?"

"I'm administering a shot now, so it won't hurt so much when it's time."

The nurse injects my medicine and disengages my wheels. The hallway she rolls me down is long, well-lit, and silent. Her hand slaps a button on the wall, and the door springs open. The technologist lowers my mattress and guardrail.

"This is the hard part. Sit up, walk over, and stand facing the equipment." The technician says, using her fingers to make a walking motion.

My breath is shallow, and the inflammation is excruciating when they help me to my feet. This is the first time since the accident that I've stood. My legs shake like jelly, and the pressure in my chest is unbearable. They don't rush me as I shuffle. Tears moisten my face as I focus straight ahead.

This is the worst pain I have ever been in, and I want to curl up and die.

They each place my palms on an elevated handle when we reach the machine. "Hold these, and don't let go. We need to stay behind the wall before taking the picture. Ready?" The nurse asks.

I nod my head and suck snot through my nostrils. The Foley catheter hanging between my legs tugs my private parts uncomfortably. The equipment makes a quiet click sound, and the staff returns to me.

"This one is a little harder. Turn to the side and grab this bar with one hand."

"Why can't I do this lying down?" I sob.

"You collapsed a lung, so diagnostically, the view is better while standing." The technician directs my hand to the upper bar and squeezes it. "Last one, I promise."

After she finished the X-rays, the technician and nurse helped me back into bed. The hospital is buzzing with activity. Patients, doctors, and visitors roam the hallways and weave in and out of rooms up and down the walkway. Super. Visiting hours have started, I think to myself. Agent Corbin will bombard me with questions again and ruin my day.

My room is empty, and I exhale through fluttering lips. Sleep is the only thing I can do. I fell asleep in no time at all. Pain is exhausting. Now I know why most of the patients at the clinic always complained about being tired.

A hand touched my shoulder, jolting me awake. A man dressed in scrubs and wearing a mask stands over me. He takes the call button away when I reach for it.

"Mia, it's me." Tony slides the mouth cover beneath his chin.

I gaze behind him at the closed door. We are alone. "Please don't hurt me." I cry as my lip quivers.

"What? I would never. I wanted to make sure you're okay."

"Why are you doing this to me? Who are you? Did you kill Nick?"

"Mia, listen to me. I need to get you out of here."

"Answer me!" I yell.

Tony puts his finger to his lips, "Shhh. Mia, stop." He strokes my hair and kisses my forehead.

"Tell me the truth." I plead.

"What is going on in here?" A nurse bursts through the door. "Who are you? I'm calling security."

Tony knocks her over as he races away. The nurse scrambles from the tile and goes after him. As chaos ensues out of sight, I weep in solitude.

After several minutes of silence, Agent Corbin enters my room.

"Mia, what happened?"

"Nothing."

"Surveillance video shows an unknown male subject entering your room. The nurse reported screaming. Did the man hurt you? Threaten you? Did you see his face?"

"No, no, and no. Please, I'm so tired."

"Mia, I'm stationing someone outside for the rest of your stay."

I keep my attention on a rip in the yellow wallpaper and ignore him. The blemish reminds me of my wall at home. I miss my place and, for some reason, the annoying cat next door.

Whenever I shut my eyes, images of Nick's brain flying at my face jar them open. I press a button tied to my bed rail.

"Yes, Mia," the nurse says, peeking in the door.

"Can I have something to knock me out?"

"Of course."

The nurse reenters with the FBI agent tasked with protecting me. He's a young man, fresh from the academy, no doubt. Despite his lack of field experience, he's attentive, observant, and serious about his assignment. The agent peers over the nurse's shoulder and examines the needle and medication she's injecting into my IV.

"I'm a nurse, not an assassin," the nurse chimes at him.

"Can't be too careful," the agent insists.

He nods at me and exits behind her. My eyes flutter and my lids become too heavy to hold open.

In my dreams, I'm home, and Mrs. Baxter and I are sharing cookies. Georgia, the kitten, is sitting on my lap and the stray who eats my trash is rubbing against Mrs. Baxter's varicose-covered leg. We rock in our chairs and stare out into the street. A car creeps closer to us, and the driver's side window rolls down. Inside, a man dressed in black points a gun at me and squeezes the trigger.

Chapter Eighteen
Code Blue

Yelling in a hospital is not something you want to wake up to, especially after having a nightmare. I should have known when I dreamt of me and Mrs. Baxter being pals, I was doomed.

Outside my room, a nurse is administering chest compressions to the young agent assigned to my room. My eyes are still crusty from sleeping, and I use my fingertips to clear the goop away.

"What happened?" I called a nurse's aide standing above them.

"Heart attack, we think, but not sure."

"What? But he's the same age as me."

The aid shrugs her shoulders as another doctor rushes beside them. The medical professionals work together to place the man on a gurney and roll him away. I gaze up at the dots on the ceiling tile. Anything can happen at any time or age, I guess. Perhaps the agent has a preexisting condition the agency missed before he joined.

The eerie silence sends chills down my spine, and I have an overwhelming urge to leave. I peer at my shaking hands, and soon my stomach shakes too. The call button is out of reach, so I rotate my arm backward to try and grab it.

A hairy hand seizes it, wraps the cord, and shoves it farther away. The man's size gives him away. He doesn't work here despite wearing scrubs. When I part my lips, he pushes his pudgy finger on them.

"Not a word," he murmurs.

I nod as he rolls a wheelchair to my bedside. His massive arms slide under me and hoist me up. I didn't mean to scream, but the pain was too much.

The man throws his palm over my mouth, "Shut up."

My knuckles whiten as I grip the sides of the rolling chair. He wheels me through the door and down the hall. A nurse rounds a corner up ahead and stops. She stares at my urine pouch dragging on the tile behind us.

"What are you doing?" she asks, picking up the bag.

"Take it out," the man orders, pointing a gun at her.

She raises her arms, stuffs her trembling hands into gloves, and grabs a sterile needle to drain the fluid at the balloon port. The catheter slides out of me, and the nurse's eyes meet mine.

"Where are you taking her?"

My captor doesn't answer. Instead, he punches her in the face, dropping her like a sack of potatoes. I gasp, then try to stand, but he takes me by the shoulders and forces me back into my seat. When the elevator opens, a real doctor stands inside and furrows his brow.

"Where are you going with my patient?" The physician asks, stepping in our path.

The man seizes the doctor by his shirt and tosses him out of the enclosed space like a weightless obstacle. As we make our descent, my life flashes before my eyes. I have a lot of regrets. There are so many things I wanted to do, foods I wanted to try, and adventures I wanted to take. They all dissipate as the elevator doors crash open and we follow the arrows on the walls leading to the parking garage.

A blacked-out SUV idles in the hospital pick-up zone. The door opens, and Carmine glares at me from the back seat. A sharp point drills into my neck as warm fluid floods through it. My body goes flaccid as the burly man heaves me next to Carmine.

"Mia, we have some things to discuss," he murmurs as a whisky glass pauses at his lips.

My head flops around on my shoulders as I try and focus on his face, but he's gazing straight ahead. "Like whom murdered my son."

When Carmine turns to me, a gnarly scar slices across his eye. The injury starts above his left eye and runs at a forty-five-degree angle to the right, stopping at his cheek. The penetrating trauma leaves him blind on one side. This is why no one can access him. The injury makes him vulnerable.

"I don't know," I slur.

"We shall see. For now, rest. We have quite a drive."

The bed I wake up in has silk sheets and plush blankets. A bell rests on the bedside, and I slide it to the floor. I'm unsure of the time, but I need to pee like crazy.

An older woman with bloodshot eyes enters wearing an apron. "Yes, Mia."

"I need to use the restroom."

"There is a bedpan," she points to the table on my other side.

"Gross. Can I try and go on my own?"

"I'm not permitted to let you up unless necessary."

"Please. I promise not to give you any trouble."

The woman sighs and glances at the closed door. "Oh, all right. I can't have you wetting the mattress. I would have to clean it."

She offers me her elbow, which I use to pull myself upright. My body sways from side to side, and she steadies me. "Don't fall, or we will both be in deep shit."

"My head is foggy."

"Tranquilizers will do that to you."

A breeze blows my hospital gown, and the woman wrinkles her nose. "Honey, you need a shower."

"No kidding."

"Well, we are in the bathroom, so we might as well kill two tasks in one shot." She says as I sit on the toilet. "Stay here and take your time. I am grabbing some supplies and an outfit."

I nod my head. Urine shoots out like Satan's blowtorch when the stream starts. I grit my teeth, stifle a scream, and hold the seat beneath me. "Oh, my god. Please make it stop."

"Mia, who are you talking to?" The woman asks, setting down towels and a washcloth.

"My pee is coming out like lava."

"Sounds about right. Are you finished?"

"Yes." I pant.

She cranks the water on and helps me ease into the bottom. Water encapsulates my fragile ribcage. I wince when she turns a handheld sprayer on and scrubs my head.

The last time someone bathed me fully was my mother years ago. Life became hard for me after she died in a car accident. My father always favored my sister, and I reminded him of her. He never treated me the same. I guess looking at me saddened him, so he ignored me.

"Lift your arms, please," the woman insists.

They almost reach the height of my shoulder's before stabbing pain forces them back down. She managed to do one quick swipe under each pit before they failed altogether.

Nick washed my back for me a few times and other places when we'd shower together. He was the first man I let my guard down with. I thought I could trust him. Boy was I wrong.

"What are you doing?" Carmine asks.

The sound of his voice startles us both. I wrap my arms around my naked breasts, and the woman puts her head down. "I'm sorry, sir. Mia needed the restroom and a bath."

He stares down at my naked frame. Having another man, any man for that matter seeing me naked is not only embarrassing but strange. He just stood there, analyzing my body.

"Dismissed." He orders the woman away.

"Yes, sir." The woman makes no eye contact as she grabs her supplies and exits.

Carmine stays silent over my exposed body. Suds pop in my hair, and the water does little to hide my skin. He rolls his sleeves up beside me and sits without a word.

Chapter Nineteen
The Boss

When his palm touches me, I flinch.

Carmine digs his fingertips into my arm. "Don't do that again. Understand?"

"Yes, sir."

He picks up a washcloth and scrubs my back. I stifle a cry when he rolls over my ribs. His hand moves around to my front. I clamp my legs shut when he tries to wash between my thighs.

Carmine yanks my knees open and pushes my rib. "What did I say?"

"I'm sorry." I cry as he continues washing my private space.

Although he didn't linger and cleaned it as a woman would, I am still uncomfortable. Nick is the only person who has ever washed me down there besides my mother and myself.

"Stand up." Carmine orders.

"I can't." I weep.

He sighs, climbs in the tub, shoes, and all, and lifts me by the armpits. One of his men comes in with his jaw dropped, and Carmine scowls at him. "Don't gawk. Help me lift her out."

Despite the man's short stature, he lifts me out with ease. He caresses the skin of my buttocks as he sets me down and smells the flesh between my breasts. Carmine's face darkens. He seizes the man by his balls and crushes them in his grasp.

"Get out!" Carmine orders as the man screams.

The man's face reddens as Carmine lets go and he leaves holding his testicles.

"My apologies, Mia."

"Sir, why am I here?"

"Nicoli's funeral is tomorrow, and he would want you to attend." Carmine huffs as he starts helping me into linen bottoms, then pauses. "And we have things to discuss."

He takes a white button-up top, shakes it, and slips my arms into it one at a time.

"What things?"

Carmine doesn't respond. Instead, he finishes buttoning my shirt and leaves the room without closing the door.

I follow him into a beautiful flower-laden courtyard. Red daylilies flank the walkway, and white roses bloom under the windows of the mansion. Two bodyguards are holding the man who touched my bottom in the bathroom. Carmine stops in front of him, pulls out a silver and black handgun, and points it at him. The pervert struggles and pleads for his life, but it's too late. Carmine squeezes the trigger, firing one round into the man's chest.

I stumbled backward, sharpening the pain in my ribcage. The wall surrounding the yard supplies support as I collect myself and slow my breathing. Nausea hovers at the surface of my esophagus as blood pools underneath his corpse onto the patio.

Carmine steps over his body and snaps his fingers. All his men line up on the walkway, their eyes fixed straight ahead.

"This is what happens when someone disrespects my guest. Do not make the same mistake. Now take him out of here before he stains my concrete."

The men each grab a limb of the lifeless man and drag him away. A curvy, crimson smear creates a path leading away to somewhere unknown. Carmine sits in an outdoor chair, and the woman who helped me bathe pours him a glass of orange juice.

"Mia, come sit," Carmine says without looking up. "It's time for breakfast."

A man stands beside me and offers help. I shake my head. Fear keeps my feet planted at the edge of a row of red roses. Carmine is watching when I glance in his direction. He rests his elbows on the table and presses his fingertips together. Irritation and impatience cast a shadow of anger across his face.

"I want to walk on my own," I announce.

"Of course," Carmine smirks as he stares at me.

My legs are heavy and uncooperative as I use various obstacles as leverage to keep me upright. The number of injuries I sustained from the accident went far beyond the fractured ribs. Nothing is working right since the accident. It's as though the force rattled every bone in my body, displacing them.

After I complained, the hospital did a full scan but found nothing significant. 'Psychological trauma can cause physical symptoms,' the doctor explained.

Everything hurts. When I reach the empty chair before Carmine, I contemplate lying on the soft grass beside him. I sit and place my folded hands on the table's surface. The woman from earlier sets a covered plate in front of me. Underneath are scrambled eggs, French toast, bacon, and a little black box.

"What's this?"

"Once Nicoli finalized his divorce, he planned to marry you right away. This is the ring he bought you." Carmine says as he opens the box.

Inside is the most beautiful ring I have ever seen. The multi-carat oval diamond is set in a gold setting with spaced-out diamonds built into the band.

The sun reflects the light into my tear-filled eyes.

"Sir, I can't accept this."

"But you are. Now put it on."

I plucked the golden circle from its white silk display and slid it on my right finger. Carmine seizes my hand with dark eyes.

"Do not insult me in my own home. Place it on the left hand where it belongs and where it will stay. No one leaves this family, married or not. No one."

He releases my hand. I take a few seconds to compose myself before rotating the ring off and sliding it with a shaking hand onto my left hand.

"Eat." Carmine orders without looking up.

"Yes, sir."

My stomach is in knots. Even though breakfast smells and looks delicious, I can't swallow a single bite. Carmine waves his fork in the air between us.

"Why aren't you eating? Are you too good to accept food from me?"

"Of course not. My stomach is upset. That's all."

Carmine shoves a slice of bacon into his mouth, tosses his napkin on the table, and stands.

"Mia, when I say it's time to eat, that's what it means. I don't care how much you manage to get down as long as I see it happen. Now, take a bite of eggs."

The fork bounces off the plate as I stab a couple of eggs and stuff them in my mouth like a spoiled brat.

"Chew," Carmine says, placing his palms face down on the tablecloth and leaning toward me.

My jaw moves up and down as I grind it up well and try to swallow. I can't. My eyes water as bile surges into my esophagus, blocking the eggs from entering my stomach.

"Swall…"

Vomit launches from my lips before Carmine could finish spitting out the word, and splatters onto the table between his outstretched hands. He moves fast, but not fast enough to avoid an overspray of liquid striking him in the shirt.

In my defense, I did tell him I wasn't feeling well.

"Fuck," he yells, peering down at his contaminated plate.

"I'm sorry."

Carmine's phone chimes in his pocket and he says nothing as he strolls away from me to answer.

Nick tried to warn me when we met. Once you become a part of his family, you are always a part of it. The term 'till death do we part' does not apply in this situation. His assassination does not free me. It holds me hostage. Nick gave me a chance to walk away when our relationship grew serious. But I loved him and ignored the bigger picture. The woman from earlier returns with a glass of orange juice, a fresh tablecloth, and a trash can. She places the entire tabletop, plates, and all, inside a garbage bag and dumps it. The scent of lemons fills the air as she sprays the table with disinfectant and places another piece of fabric on top.

"I'm sorry."

"Don't be sorry. He shouldn't have pushed you to eat when you weren't feeling well."

"How did you know?"

She rests her hand on my arm. "There are cameras everywhere, dear. Be careful what you say and do, okay?"

I nod as I pan the courtyard for surveillance equipment. On the wall, near the entrance to the house, a black box shifts from right to left with a green light illuminated on its top. I didn't notice it before. Carmine isn't the only one watching.

She starts walking away, but I stop her. "Excuse me. Where is Mrs. Castino?"

Her eyes look away from me as she focuses on the ground. "Oh my. You didn't hear?" She glances over her shoulder and shakes her head. "Sophie passed away over a month ago."

"What? How?"

The fabric of her apron wrinkles as she crumples it in her grasp.

"Well, she suffered a seizure caused by a brain aneurysm. The doctors did everything they could, but she died after a few months in a coma. Nick and Carmine didn't handle it so well. None of us did." She hangs her head, and a tear drips onto the ground.

"I'm sorry. I didn't mean to upset you."

"After you left Nick, his entire world came crashing down. Now I don't blame you for what's happened, but others may. Watch your back young lady."

She hustles away as Carmine approaches me, wearing a new shirt. He sits across from me and pulls his sleeves down. It's hot and humid, but he doesn't break a sweat. I wish I could be so lucky. Beads of salty liquid glide down my spine, tickling it. They increase in volume, as he glares across the table at me. The top of my pants is uncomfortable and wet with perspiration. I can't hide my tears, sadness, or guilt. No more than I can sit here and sweat while he intimidates me without saying a word.

I lift my head, stare into Carmine's one working eye, and ask, "Are you going to kill me?"

Chapter Twenty
Funeral

Carmine gulps his orange juice in its entirety and slams the glass down on the table. He stares at the empty container for a long time. When he lifts his head to face me, there is a hint of sorrow lingering in his expression.

"Mia, if I wanted to kill you, you'd be dead already."

The woman returns to Carmine's side. A slight breeze carries a smoky smell from her clothing into my nostrils. The scent is familiar, but I can't place it. Perhaps something from my past. A bonfire when I was in high school or a bar patron who came into Stevie's. Carmine wiggles his nose and gives her a disapproving glare.

"This is Blaire. Anything you need, ask her, and she can get it for you. Right now, change your clothes. The funeral is in a couple of hours."

Blaire nods her head upward and to the side. I stand and walk with slow steps behind her. The room we enter has several black dresses hanging from a mobile clothing rack. A few sets of bras and underwear are on a dresser nearby. On the floor are three pairs of heels.

"Choose a dress, shoes, and your undergarments. I can help you with your hair."

"My hair?" I say, turning to the full-length mirror.

My blonde locks are a jumbled pile of crushed, curly, frizzy, and straight pieces. Multiple sections stick up in every direction but down.

"Quite the mess isn't it," Blaire says as she fluffs my head from behind. "But I can fix anything."

"Can you fix my situation?"

"Honey, I want to keep my head, if you know what I mean," she huffs at my reflection.

I stare at the solid oak floors beneath my bare feet. The red polish on my toes is chipping on the ends, and small dirt smudges run around the edges of my feet from walking barefoot in the courtyard. Blaire grimaces and opens a cabinet on the far wall. She motions for me to sit in a chair and scrubs my toenails with acetone.

After all signs of paint vanish, she cleans my feet and repaints my nails with a shimmering gold color.

"Thank you, Blaire."

"No problem."

Blaire moves behind me and brushes my hair. She holds it one section at a time and runs the bristles through, careful not to pull. A hot iron beeps, and she curls from one side of my head to the other. She applies a small amount of makeup to rosy up my cheeks and hide the bruising.

She places two sets of footwear before me, has me put one of each on, and rotates her head from one to the other.

"The one with the crisscross straps, for sure."

I turn and face my reflection. The black, backless zip-up rests off the shoulders and hugs just below the knee. Blaire passes me oversized sunglasses and a small handbag.

"What's inside?"

"Tissues, ChapStick, and hand sanitizer," Blaire smiles. "Time to go."

Two men with handguns under their blazers open the front door. Carmine is waiting beside an SUV. One of many. Seven, to be precise. He offers me his palm and aids me into the vehicle.

"Despite this solemn day, there are beautiful things to gaze upon."

"The roses are amazing," I smile and admire the various hybrids planted on either side of the mansion entryway."

"I'm not talking about the flowers, Mia."

"Oh. Ummm. Thanks."

The procession leaves the property and drives down a tree-lined, paved road. When we reach the end, a massive gate swings outward, and men with automatic weapons allow our exit. The walls around the acreage went on for miles. High, white concrete fortified barriers with metal spikes surrounded

Carmine's compound. A jeep drives by with guards in bulletproof vests patrolling the outskirts. They nod at our driver as we pass.

Carmine is quiet. Loneliness and loss emanate from his body, tugging at my heart. No one should have to bury their one and only child.

I rest my hand on his and give it a gentle squeeze. It's my way of apologizing without saying the words to upset him further. He takes his hand away and wipes it on his pants as though I contaminated his skin.

The SUV parks at a private family cemetery. Nick's coffin sits next to a deep hole in the earth. His mother's grave is a few feet away. Carmine's birthdate and a dash etched beside her date of death.

The other vehicles unload. People in dark shades and morbid attire surround the clergy. After he puts Nick's body into the ground, a eulogist speaks fond memories of Nick. Each of us takes a long stem rose and tosses it onto his mahogany and gold-trimmed casket.

A woman pauses within a foot of me and removes her sunglasses. Her eyes are fierce and bloodshot.

"You killed him. This is your fault," she seers.

"I didn't. I…"

She slaps me across the cheek before the next word escapes my mouth. Carmine seizes her wrist as I raise my fist, but Blaire pulls me away by the waist, crushing my painful rib. I'm unsure what he said, but her face lost color. When he lets go, one of his men yanks her by the upper arm and forces her into an idle vehicle.

Carmine stops at the edge of his son's resting place and tosses in the final rose. Mourners file back into their transportation and drive back to the mansion.

My fingers rotate around each other as I wait for him to join us. He's talking to himself. I imagine he's saying all the things he regretted not saying to Nick before he died. Carmine shakes the eulogist's hand and strolls toward us.

Blaire takes my hand and grimaces. "No matter what he says, just apologize."

Carmine slides in beside me, and a long, irritating blast of air escapes his nose. I rub my unused knuckles and wish I could be anywhere else but here.

"Mia, what Rosie did, won't happen again. She's mourning the loss of her husband and believes you're responsible for his death. Though not together, they stayed friends. I know you intended to strike her in response. I'm pleased Blaire prevented you from acting, for the consequences would have been painful."

"I meant no disrespect, sir. I'm sorry."

"Mia, stop calling me sir. From now on, call me Carmine."

I'm not family, so what has changed? Only close friends and relatives can address him by name. I am neither. Words hang unspoken in the air, making it hard to breathe.

Everyone in this SUV knows what they are—everyone except for me.

Chapter Twenty-One
The will

The drive to the mansion couldn't end soon enough. I retreat to a vacant sunroom and pick a book from a side table.

Inside is a plain white tattered bookmark, with a single silver bead attached to a silky string, and a personalized message. 'I love you, mom. Love, Nicoli.' A smile tugs at the corner of my mouth as Carmine sits beside me.

"What are you doing?"

"I'm sorry. I like reading, so I…." I set the paperback back where I found it and placed my hands on my lap. "It isn't mine, so I shouldn't have touched it. I apologize."

"I'm not talking about the novel. You can read whatever you like. I mean, why are you in here?"

"I'm uncomfortable around people I don't know."

"They aren't strangers, Mia. They're family."

The crowd in the next room is unrelated and irrelevant to me. I have no connection to them, nor do I want it.

In my mind, I think about Tony. He said I'm in danger, but I never let him tell me how. I wish I had listened.

"But I'm not family," I say, rejoining the conversation.

"Mia, my son chose you, and by doing so, he made you a part of this family." He stands and extends his palm to me. "Come. It's time for you to meet everyone."

Carmine marches me through a massive crowd. One by one, he introduces me to all his family and friends.

An older woman hugs me and smiles at Carmine. "Beautiful girl. Welcome to the family."

I nod but remain quiet. My insides are shaking, and I want to run. A small child runs at me, stops, and hugs my thighs. His lashes remind me of Nick's, long and dark. His mother apologizes and drags him away.

Nearby a tall, tan, dark-haired guy with a slight grey streak on either side of his head is listening to the person beside him. He undresses me with his eyes as he excuses himself and closes in on Carmine and me.

I can't breathe, speak, think, or move when the man stands in front of us. He takes my hand and kisses it but doesn't let go. Carmine removes my hand from his and turns me away from them both. I didn't catch what Carmine said to him, but the man left within minutes of their conversation.

"Who is he?" I ask Carmine when he returns to my side.

"Someone you'll never see again." He says as he finishes off his bourbon.

A man in a suit nods to him, and he does the same. "Stay close to Blaire." He orders as he strolls away.

An argument comes from the closed doors within minutes, and Nicoli's wife storms out. A fresh bandage covers the hand she struck me with, and she's crying. She and I make brief eye contact before she throws the entryway door open and slams it behind her.

The room fell quiet for a few seconds then everyone continued talking. Carmine punished Nick's wife for making a scene at his son's gravesite. I wonder if her childish display this time will earn her another reprimand or worse.

Blaire presses through two people and grabs my hand. "Come with me."

"Why? What's the matter?"

Blaire does not respond. Instead, she leads me through the office doorway and shuts me in. Carmine and a man dressed in a well-tailored, three-piece gray suit are leaning against an oak desk. In front of them are two red velvet Victorian chairs.

"Sit down," Carmine orders. "This gentleman is the family attorney.".

The lawyer pulls a sheet of paper from behind his back and adjusts his wireframes. "To my only true love, Mia Galano, I leave the second half of my monetary assets." The round, stout man removes his glasses and rubs the bridge of his nose. "Miss

Galano, Nicoli wished his funds to be split between yourself and Carmine."

"What?"

"Congratulations, you're rich." The attorney smiles and hands me a manila envelope. "After you fill these out, give them to Carmine, and I can take care of the rest."

The attorney shakes Carmine's hand and exits the room. I slide the pile of paperwork from its sleeve. On the front page, the estimated net assets are over six million. My cut is a few thousand over three million.

Nick had a knack for business, but I wasn't aware of how well he did until now. I never asked. It didn't matter to me. Money never did.

"I don't want this." I proclaim, setting the papers on the seat beside me.

"Nicoli loved you. These are his wishes."

"What about his wife? This should go to her, shouldn't it?"

"He left her the house and his cars. Their value is more and satisfies his obligation to her."

"So, I fill this out, and this is all mine?"

"Correct."

With this amount, I can buy a house wherever I want. The mountains are beautiful, but I love the ocean, and traveling so maybe an oceanside home in Italy. The possibilities are endless.

"And I can go home?"

"Home? Mia, this is your home."

"No, I live upstate and have to return to work."

"Not anymore. The lawyer sent your two former employers a resignation letter by express mail."

"What are you talking about? I need to go back. I have things at my house, and what about my car?" I stand and back away from him.

"On the other side of the property is a garage full of cars and SUVs for you to choose from. As for your property, I have men picking it up as we speak."

"I don't want to live here," I argue.

Carmine charges me from the desk, grabs me by the arms, and brings his face so close to mine, I smell the bourbon on his breath. "I have lost my wife, my son and have no heirs to continue my legacy. You are staying here. I'm your family now, and this is our home."

'Our'

The word hung in the air like a lingering stench. Pain surges through my chest and midsection as he wraps his palms around my upper body and applies pressure to my fragile cage.

"Pleeeeeaaaase, stop," I scream as he forces me back into the chair.

Tears cascade over my cheeks as Carmine's face twists. He glances at his hands and eases them off my center and onto my belly.

"You will be my wife and provide me with a son. If you reject my request, I will exile you from the family."

And there it is. The big reveal. This is why I am here. To be his vessel. To be his surrogate wife.

"Well, exile me. I don't want to marry you." I hiss.

He grabs my face, closes his eyes, and presses his nose against mine. "Mia, no one leaves. Remember?"

"What are you saying?" I whisper.

My heart pounds as his eyes open, and he backs away. His palms push off my thighs as he stands and glares at me. The darkness in them gives me the answer, but I still wait for it.

"If you leave, you die."

Chapter Twenty-Two
Rules

Carmine removes a familiar notebook from his desk. He rests the black book with gold lettering on the side table beside me.

His knees crack as he kneels before me and places his palms on my tremoring hands. I pull away, and he grips them.

"Nicoli mentioned he tried to give you this, but you refused. Number seven is significant. You should review it first." Carmine releases me, stands, and turns his back as he walks away. "The rules didn't matter to you then, but I bet they do now," he says over his shoulder.

Footsteps dissipate as he exits the room and closes the door. My fingers caress the rule book's leather cover. The day Nick asked me to read it came flooding back to me. I told him I didn't need to if we were together. How foolish was I? How could I have been so blind?

If I hadn't seen Nick crush a man's skull, I wouldn't have left, and he would still be alive. Before that day, Nick had never conducted business in my presence. We were out to eat when he spotted the man having dinner alone. The man took off when he and Nick made eye contact.

I stayed at the table at first, but too much time passed, and I became worried, so I walked outside to find him. All the men froze when I rounded the corner of the alley behind the restaurant, except for Nick. He didn't see me at first as his alligator boots stomped on the man's head over and over. After a brief struggle, one of his men seized his arms and whispered to him.

He didn't turn in my direction right away. There was a long pause as though he didn't dare see the disappointment on my face. When he did have the courage to face me, his eyes changed from dark and angry to regret and sadness.

Nick chased me down the street that night and explained it was just business. Taking someone's life is more than that to me. Nick played judge, jury, and executioner. If the man owed him money, and now he is dead, how is what he did going to make a difference?

I return my attention to the book I'm holding and open it. Inside are laminated expectations for the women.

#7 Any available woman shall be joined in matrimony to a direct family member needing a spouse. An opposing family is allowed under most circumstances to ask for the hand of the woman to combine financial and strategic power between the two families.

Blaire enters the room and sets a drink on the desk for me. The list slides off my lap to the floor.

"Blaire, who was the man who came to the party. He tried to introduce himself and held my hand."

"The sharks are circling, Mia. The man Carmine asked to leave is from another family. His fiancé disappeared last year."

"Disappeared? Like murdered or?"

"Honey, I don't know, and I'm not planning to ask. All I know is he got cold feet. His father was disappointed of course. This is the second time he's been engaged and bowed out before the wedding. He likes prancing around, enjoying the single life. At least he did, until today. I haven't seen him in some time. He heard about you and came to see what's on the menu." Blaire peered over her shoulder, verifying the door was closed. "Carmine has no interest in fighting over you. If anyone comes calling, they will be turned away regardless of the consequences."

"What consequences?"

"No more questions. Finish reading and meet me in the sunroom in an hour."

Blaire hustles out of the room. The open book mocks me from the floor as I sob. The one time I chose not to read, I should have. Rules are important, especially in this twisted lifestyle.

The rest of the list is common sense, except for the last one.

#10 Do not harm another member unless they violate the above rules.

Nick's wife violated rules three and number ten.

#3 Do not make or cause a scene in public or a place that may draw unwanted attention from authorities.

The cemetery is family-owned, but it is on a public road. Anyone watching saw her strike me, and she didn't have the authority. Only the man the woman is promised to or married to can decide their fate.

Nick not only hurt me because he was off his meds but because I violated number one.

#1 Once brought into the family, no one leaves. Violation of this rule without permission is punishable by death or an equivalent reprimand.

Perhaps Nick left me to his father in his will like a piece of property as punishment. Carmine isn't a bad-looking guy. Except for his scar, a few extra pounds, and being twenty years older, he is an aged Nick. But I don't want another version of Nick. I want to go home.

Blaire mentioned consequences if anyone objects to him keeping me to himself. It could be a way out. The man who kissed my hand may be able to help me. It could buy me some time if I could turn him and Carmine against each other and create a rift between the families.

No one can leave may be a rule, but I have broken it once and survived. Doing it a second time may be harder, but still possible. Staying here is not an option. I have responsibilities and jobs to get home to. When Stevie receives my resignation, he will no doubt panic and have a meltdown. Not to mention my boss at the clinic. I'm his favorite employee. There must be a way to get a message to them that I am being held against my will.

As if Carmine realized he never said it to me, he enters the room and towers over me. I keep my eyes on the floor, and he takes my face and lifts it to him.

"Mia, before you get any ideas, you should know the consequences. If anyone tries to come take you from me, they will die. If you try and send a message out to anyone or contact the authorities, I will kill everyone you know. Your father, your estranged sister, friends, coworkers, and even your neighbor, Mrs. Baxter, will all meet an untimely death. Are we clear?"

"Yes, sir."

"I told you before, call me Carmine."

"Yes, Carmine."

Something catches his attention out the window, and he leaves the room. I slide out of my chair and gaze out into the courtyard. The man from the funeral is stepping out of his car. Carmine is pointing and yelling at him as the man puts his hands up.

"Get away from the window," one of Carmine's men hollers from the doorway startling me.

"What are they arguing about?"

"None of your business. Now move."

I return to my seat and finish reading the paperwork from the attorney. Carmine's signature is above the line where mine goes. I grab a pen, then hesitate. I didn't read the rule book before, and I should have. Now is not the time to ignore important documents because millions are floating in my face. I took the time to read it, and I am happy I did. In the fine print, tucked in between a bunch of legal jargon, was a pregnancy clause. It simply says when I have a male heir, all monies belonging to me will transfer at once to a trust in the child's name. If a female child is born first, ten percent will be entrusted to her. If it takes more than two tries to produce a male heir, the percentage reduces to five. I would receive nothing regardless.

I take a red ink pen from the top of the desk and make notes in the margin.

Change to equal shares for all children regardless of gender before the age of eighteen. Men should not be valued higher than women. Not ever. We are equal under the eyes of God and therefore should be treated as such.
Mia Galano.

I rest the paper on the desk and smile. A colorful assortment of push-pin tacks rests in a glass dish. I pinch one between my thumb and pointer finger and stab the paper into the unblemished wood surface. I'm sure Carmine will punish me for this later, but it was worth it to get my point across.
Point.
I giggle at my own joke as Carmine's guy returns to escort me to the sunroom.

Chapter Twenty-Three
A Familiar Face

The sunroom is my favorite place to hang out in the mansion. Its expansive collection of books and comfortable furniture supply a cozy and peaceful atmosphere. If I'm stuck here, I might as well take advantage of the fancy lifestyle.

Blaire is waiting for me as I enter and motions for me to sit beside her.

She pours me a glass of lemonade with ice and one for herself.

"Mia, I know this is hard, but you must understand. The family legacy is all that matters to Carmine. In his mind, the only choice he has is for you two to wed and have a son. He's not getting any younger, so the window of opportunity is closing."

"Blaire, can I do anything to get out of this?"

"Short of keeling over? No." Blaire stands and closes the sunroom door. "If you are thinking of leaving, think again. Carmine is always watching."

"I need to leave the house. I've been stuck inside for days."

"You are still recovering, but I'm sure something can be arranged."

Blaire pats me on the forearm and strolls away. The lemonade puckers my lips as I sit and pick up a magazine. Why is everyone in magazines so happy? It's unrealistic. Life isn't all about cooking, home decor, and uplifting stories. The real world is harsh, cruel, and twisted. At least, to me, it is.

Carmine comes through the entryway buttoning his shirt. Behind him, two of his soldiers dressed all in black await his orders.

"Mia, these two gentlemen are my most trusted men. They are taking you shopping for a lunch date and dinner party we are attending tonight."

"What do I need to wear?"

"Something blue." He sits beside me. "I would come with you, but I have a more pressing matter."

If I can run away from them, I may have a chance.

"Mia, did you read the rules?"

"Yes."

"And you understand what will happen if you break them?"

"I think so."

"I'm glad." Carmine rests his hand on my thigh. "I wouldn't want to have to punish you."

A shiver shot threw my hips and exited the front of my legs. The more I'm around this man, the more I am concerned about my safety. One of the guys fully enters the room and waits after Carmine leaves. I tried to ignore him, but his presence annoyed me, so I gave up on relaxing.

The silver SUV caught me off guard. Carmine's entire fleet is black. I turn to Blaire, and she nods.

"It's more discreet than shopping with multiple cars," she says as she places her hand on the small of my back and helps me climb in.

"Aren't you coming?"

"No, I have to prepare tonight's meal."

The vehicle is a seven-passenger full-size machine. Inside, five men, not two, crowded the space. Body odor penetrates and singes my nose hairs with its putrid scent. I roll the window down halfway, and the driver rolls it back up.

"Air conditioning is on. Leave it up." He shouts from the front.

"Well, if I don't have fresh air, I'm throwing up on this man's lap beside me."

The man next to me scoots away. He smacks the driver's shoulder and furrows his brow. I don't blame him. I wouldn't want someone to vomit on me, either. The sad part is I think he's the one who forgot deodorant today.

The glass glides down a quarter of the way. I lift my nose to the partial opening and take a deep breath.

The streets have multiple shops and eateries to choose from. People mill about on the sidewalks, oblivious of the danger rolling past them. The five-armed escorts I travel with have two jobs, keeping me safe and preventing me from leaving. Anyone who threatens their mission dies. Collateral damage be damned.

We parked beside a storefront, and I let myself out. Two men station themselves on either side of me. One lingers in the front and one behind. The driver doesn't go anywhere in case we need to make a quick exit.

A dress on a mannequin catches my attention at once. The royal blue beauty is long-sleeved, with a twist beneath the breasts, and stops at the knee. A salesperson removes it at my request and walks me down a narrow hallway and around the corner to the dressing rooms. The guard checks the door nearby, and it's locked. No way out. The one bodyguard nods for the others to go as he stands outside the curtain.

I slip off my sandals, pull the dress up from the bottom, and slide it over my shoulders. The silk hugs my curves in all the right places and enhances my blue eyes.

The canvas partition sways inward as grunting comes from the other side. The rings holding the material clank as I threw the fabric out of my field of vision.

Warm liquid tosses across my face as a man all in black slices the bodyguard's neck. The close quarters prevent my escape as the murderer stands before me and removes his mask.

"Mia, it's me."

I couldn't move, breathe, or speak as Tony used his thumbs to smudge the blood from my cheeks. Red fluids puddle beneath my feet as Tony's words echo far away. The man's empty eyes stared through me from the floor.

"Listen, I'm coming for you. Do you understand? Mia?"

Like someone choking on a hotdog, a weird noise comes from inside my throat as I try to talk.

"Don't let him have you. He'll be dead soon. They all will." Tony whispers as he cranks his face to meet mine. "Mia, resist his advances at all costs. Nod if you can hear me."

I'm stuck somewhere between awake and passed out on the floor beside the lifeless corpse outside my dressing room stall. Tony hugs me, but I don't reciprocate. He goes to say something more when the screaming begins.

The salesperson rounds the corner and takes off in the opposite direction, continuing to wail as she bolts down the hallway. Tony kisses me hard on the lips and disappears behind the locked door. Carmine's men stop at once when they almost trip on their associate lying on the tile. One of them reaches for me, and I remain motionless.

The man tries a second time to get me to move, but I refuse. He lifts me up and over the dead body as I scream. Not only because of my painful ribs, but because this is the second time someone's bodily fluids have launched across my face. I can't take it anymore. Bodies keep piling up around me, and based on what Tony said, there are more to come. I flop in the bodyguard's arms, and he drops me into the grass between the sidewalk and the street. I didn't even realize we were outside the store. It's like the universe launched me from one dimension to the next in a time warp. He leans down to grab me, but I scoot away.

"Don't do this, Mia. We need to go. Right now, you haven't done anything wrong. But if you run, the boss will hurt you. He'll hurt us all. Now please, let me help you."

I rub my elbows with my opposing palms. He's right. As much as I want to get away from them, Carmine will find me. And when he does, the punishment may be worse than death. People passing by begin stopping and watching the interaction between myself and this group of men. I'm drawing attention to us, breaking rule number three. If I run, I violate rule number seven as well. Death is a certainty.

This time, when he offers me his hand, I take it with a half-hearted smile. The concerned onlookers' faces soften as I slide into the backseat. Carmine's guy hops in beside me.

"Thank you, Mia. I didn't want to die today."

We pull away from the curb and drive in the direction of home. I wonder what his name is as he sits beside me and bites his lip. Even though he kept me safe and prevented my escape, he may still receive punishment. Perhaps since he's one of Carmine's most trusted employees, he will spare him. I have my doubts after what I have seen thus far. This may be the last time I will ever smell or see him, which is fine by me.

Chapter Twenty-Four
Silence

The drive back is a complete blank. A portal picks us up from the shop and drops us in the driveway in front of the mansion. The time in between dropped into a black hole.

Blaire whips the door open and covers her mouth. Her finger wraps a lock of hair over my ear.

"Mia?"

She twists her face at my pale, tainted appearance and vanishes. Nothing is real. This can't be happening to me. I'm beside myself, wondering what my problem is. Who is this weak imposter sitting where I should be? Is she who I was always meant to be?

The pounding in my heart reaches my head and pierces through my temple like an icepick. I hold my ribs and rock like a pendulum without trying. My eyes twitch, one then the other, back, and forth.

Carmine appears with furrowing brows. He turns my face to him, but I don't recognize him. My eyes peer past him at the roses by the doorway. His finger enters his mouth and swipes at the crimson stains on my cheek.

It's fine. Everything is fine. I've only seen two people murdered before my eyes and a pile of dead bodies in the last several days. Now the man responsible for kidnapping me from the hospital is using his spit to remove his employee's blood from my face. I'm becoming numb to the violence. Soon it will be normal, like swatting irritating flies away from your food.

"Blaire, draw a bath at once," Carmine orders.

His one hand slides under my thighs and the other behind my back. I don't object, scream, or fight despite the excruciating pain when he swoops me out of the car. His feet squeak across the marble floors as he brings me to a massive master bathroom. The waterfall rages into the claw foot tub as he sets me on a velvet bench beside it.

Blaire rolls a wheeled stool before me and uses a plush wet white washcloth to cleanse the blood. Carmine waits until she removes my soiled dress, lifts me, and places me in the hot bath. He passes her a new cloth and a container of body wash.

A phone chimes inside his pocket, and he steps away to answer. The water turns transparent rust as the stains on my skin vanish. Blaire drains the discolored liquid and refills the tub with fresh. The removable shower head blasts my scalp as she washes it one-handed.

Carmine motions Blaire to his side. They whisper inaudible words a few feet away. After a short argument, Blaire leaves.

He sits in silence beside me and rubs his face with his hands. "Mia, who did this?"

If I could speak, I wouldn't have. Any enemy of Carmine is a friend to me. Or, in this case, a lover. Tony is coming to save me and kill them all. The less Carmine is aware of, the better. Seeing Nick stomp a man from a distance is one thing, but watching Tony slice a man's throat right in front of me is another.

Though their reasons for killing differ, I hesitate to trust anyone capable of such violence without batting a lash. Tony has tormented and stalked me for weeks, but I don't think he would ever hurt me. I should be furious. Instead, every time I open my mouth to lay into him for what he has done, I clam up, and my heart softens. When he touches me, I can feel his tenderness coming straight from his heart into mine. Something is wrong with me. Perhaps something is wrong with us both.

Carmine intends to force me into marriage and motherhood. I won't let it happen, no matter what the consequences may be.

"Mia!" Carmine raises his voice, bringing my attention back to the room. "Tell me."

"Sir, please." Blaire bursts into the room. "Give her some time. She's traumatized."

He hangs his head beside me and shakes it. Tears blend with suds on my face as Carmine swirls the water by my feet and pulls the plug. Goosebumps cover every inch of me as the vortex of tainted water rotates down the drain and vanishes. The tub is empty, and so am I.

Carmine reaches for me. I don't flinch as he strokes my shoulders. "I'm sorry."

He could say 'sorry' for the rest of his life, and it would still be superficial. His words aren't sincere. They come across as forceful and shallow when he blurts them out. He doesn't mean it.

Knuckles wrap on the door, and he lets out a frustrated breath. "Not now!" Carmine screams, and I jump.

His phone rings again, and he launches it at the wall putting a massive hole in it. "No more interruptions. No more calls."

Blaire stands up, holding the towel meant to dry me.

He seizes it from her. "Out."

She frowns at his tantrum. "But sir, I think it…."

"Out!" He shouts in her face.

She huffs out of the room and slams the door behind her. Carmine lifts me out and carries me into his bedroom. I didn't realize it then, but they never removed my undergarments when they put me in the tub.

Carmine sits me on the edge of the bed and unhooks my bra. I tremble beneath his touch as he pats my breasts dry. He eases my almost naked frame into a lying position and removes my wet underwear. I curl into a ball, trying to hide my private parts from him. He sighs and shakes his head.

I'm compliant when he separates my legs and dries between them while I cry. When he finishes, I tuck my hands between my legs. My muscles tighten around me in a defensive position. I am completely vulnerable.

"I will never force myself on you, Mia. But when the time is right, I expect you to say yes." His gaze is unwavering as he covers me to my neck with a plush blanket. "We can talk more about what happened and our future later. For now, get some rest."

The front of his dress pants bulges with an enormous erection that's difficult to ignore. Undressing and bathing me turned him on, but he is restraining his desire for another time. He retreats to a desk on the other side of the room and sits in a chair facing me. My body is slow to relax, but when it finally does, exhaustion takes its place.

The lighting in the room dims as he presses buttons on a laptop. Carmine's silhouette is all that is visible. Even though I can no longer see him, I can feel him, watching me from the shadows. His breaths pierce the silence and speak volumes. He's angry. Not only at me but at the situation, the loss of his men, and the need growing between his legs. He wants me, and soon I will have no choice but to let him have me.

"Close your eyes, Mia."

There is no face, and no other sounds—a mere voice in the darkness of this blackened room giving me a direct order.

I comply but do not sleep. I listen to his quiet breathing. Perhaps he is doing the same. Waiting for me to pass out so he, too, can relax. Footsteps close in on me, and my body stiffens. The floor creaks before me, and the bed shifts under his weight as he sits beside me. His hand travels across my forearm and stops on the side of my head.

"I'm sorry," he whispers into the dark space between us.

This time he means it. I sense his relief with finally saying something meaningful. Sometimes the sincerest apology comes when you least expect it. Not in the heat of the moment or after a tedious argument. But when all is quiet, and the night is still. It breaches the silence between us and fills my eyes with tears as I feel its truth.

I made no reply. What could I possibly say that would change how he feels about me or me about him? Nothing. He has made his choice, and I have none, so what's the point? I'm not even sure what he's sorry about, hurting me or forcing me to be his wife and bear his child. Perhaps because he can't see me, the message is meant more for the wife he lost.

Carmine clears his nose and removes his palm. The mattress shifts up, and his fingers slide down my hip as he moves toward the footboard. The blanket shifts off my shoulder as he climbs in bed beside me and covers himself. He doesn't touch me, but I can sense he wants to. Within minutes, soft snoring comes from behind me. I close my tear-filled eyes and drift into a light sleep.

Chapter Twenty-Five
Talk

When I wake up, an arm is around my waist, and bare flesh touches my backside. Air staggers from my lungs as I try to move away.

Carmine draws me closer and brushes his hand across my nipple on its way to my neck.

"Morning." Carmine yawns as his fingers caress my throat. "Don't worry. Nothing happened. I sleep naked all the time."

His palm travels down my ribs, over my waist, and stops on my thigh. Fingers grip me tight as Carmine grinds himself against me from behind.

"I can't wait to have you," Carmine whispers. "It has been so long for me."

After yesterday, who would have thought he would wake up in such a mood?

"Last night was the first time, in a long time, that I have slept." He sniffs the back of my neck. "Your smell reminds me of her."

His now rock-hard cock presses against my buttocks, and I shift forward. He seizes me hard, pulling me back to him. "Don't move."

The only way to stop a man in a certain mood is to change the subject to something unsavory.

"He's coming to kill you all," I blurt as I grit my teeth and wince, preparing for his reaction.

Carmine stops touching me at once. He flips me onto my spine, climbs on top, and pins me to the bed.

"Who, Mia?"

"I don't know," I hiss.

"Liar!" Carmine shouts in my face. "Tell me the truth."

"I am."

"Want to lie to me? You're breaking the rules, Mia. The punishment is what I chose, so I suggest you start talking," Carmine insists as his hand travels between his legs.

"Talk, or else," he warns as he caresses the inside of my upper thigh with his fingertips.

My head shakes, not willing to reveal Tony's name. Carmine takes his manhood in his hand and makes circles around my opening with it. "I'm a man with needs, Mia."

Circling closer…

"Talk." Carmine hums.

Closer…

I need to tell him something, or he means to take me. A version of the truth to answer his question but not give up Tony in the process.

Touching the outside…

"I'm not sure who he is, but he killed Nick."

Carmine's face changes, and he stops his advances. I didn't lie. I don't know Tony, but he wants Carmine and his family dead.

He snatches me by the hair and flips me onto my stomach. Pain shoots through my tender ribs as he mounts my back and pulls my head backward.

"If I find out you're lying, I'll fuck you in every opening you have. Do you understand?"

"Yes," I murmur as he dismounts and walks away.

A massive tattoo of a fire-breathing dragon is on his back. His butt and Nicks are the same. What a strange thing to inherit from your father, I think as I weep.

When he turns around, I notice his manhood is not something Nick inherited. This curved monstrosity is something I wouldn't wish on my worst enemy.

He leans his naked rear against his desk and picks up the phone. "Is it clean?" A long pause breaks up his sentences. "Bring it in."

Blaire walks in with the blue dress on a hanger a few minutes later. She averts her eyes at once when she realizes Carmine is bare.

"Oh, dear." Blaire gasps and hands him the outfit. "If you need anything else, holler."

The dress dangles from Carmine's finger as he approaches me. His soft shaft swings before him.

Carmine stops beside me and lays the silky attire on the comforter. "Put it on."

"No."

"Now," he orders.

"What about underwear and a bra?"

"No. I want you to be uncomfortable and accessible. Tonight, the truth shall come out. And if you are lying, I am taking you where you stand, regardless of who is around. If you prefer to tell me everything at any point today, I may spare you, or I may not."

A tear escapes my lid. Carmine swipes it with his pointer, takes it into his mouth, and sucks it off. I cringe at the thought of his lips touching me.

A soft knock at the door breaks his intense stare. He stuffs his arms into a robe, ties it, and opens the door. Blaire waltzes in as Carmine walks out, leaving us alone. My legs fail, and I collapse on the floor in despair.

Blaire rushes to my side and lifts my chin. "Tell him the truth. I've seen what he can do to those who disobey."

"I'm scared," I whispered to her. "He said he will take me if I don't tell him everything."

"Carmine would never. It is an empty threat. He's trying to scare you into spilling your guts."

"But he came so close already. He…"

"Mia, trust me. He won't. Carmine can be ruthless, and he may strike you or kill you, but he's not a rapist."

"Thanks, Blaire. I feel much better now."

"Sometimes death is better," Blaire sighs.

The sadness in her eyes is evidence of a long and daunting career with a ruthless and violent boss. Instead of offering me comfort, she exhales an exhausted breath.

"Let's put this dress on."

"Why is he making me wear it?"

"To remind you of what happened and the man he lost."

Blaire fixes my hair and applies makeup to my bruises. She opens a jewelry box, removes a sapphire and white gold choker, and wraps it around my throat. The weight of it pulls at the back of my neck.

"It's beautiful," I say, stroking its diamond accents.

Blair smiles at my reflection and pats my shoulder.

"You remind him of her," She sniffles. "And me too."

"Do we look that much alike?"

"Well, yes and no. Your hair is the same, and your eye color, of course. I think it's just a combination of things. You have likes and dislikes that are similar."

"Why are there no photos of her?"

"Carmine made us remove all of them after she passed. They were too hard for him to look at."

"That's sad."

"I keep one in my purse behind the emergency cash in my wallet," she smiles and hands me the image.

Sophie's frame is smaller than mine, but our facial features are similar in some ways. She's sitting in the sunroom reading with glasses resting below the bridge of her nose.

I pass the image back to Blaire, and she tucks it in her purse.

"Carmine was a good and fair man once, but time and circumstances have changed him. He's not the man I used to know. When Sophie died, it hardened him further, making it difficult for anyone to get close to him. Nicoli's death sent him on a violent path of destruction worse than I have ever seen. Choose your words wisely. His finger is on the trigger, and I'd hate for you to be in the crossfire when he pulls it."

"I understand."

"I hope so," Blaire says, raising her eyebrow. "Come. Let's not keep him waiting.

"Where are we going?"

"He didn't say. Which worries me."

"Great. Now I'm worried."

Carmine and a car are waiting when she leads me outside. He leans over and kisses my cheek as I shudder. "Beautiful girl."

A fake smile manifests across my face as he places his hand on my spine and ushers me into his backseat.

The ride is quiet, and Carmine doesn't offer up where we are heading. We wind our way up a hill and stop at an iron gate. Whoever lives here doesn't have the same level of security as Carmine. The driver presses a button and announces our arrival.

The divide screeches open as we roll forward. A chalet with massive windows and an enormous, elevated decking is ahead when I glance through the windshield. A few parked vehicles sit outside, but there are no other signs of life. The pit in my abdomen grows as we close in on the abandoned place.

"Where are we?"

Carmine says nothing as we park by a windowless door beneath an overlook. The man from the mansion with the gray streaks in his hair appears from the other side of the house.

My door opens, and I turn to Carmine. "What the hell is happening?"

"Out," he orders without looking at me.

"No," I say as my eyes widen. "Why?"

"I'm tired of telling you everything twice," he huffs. "Now get out of the car."

"No!"

I ignore Blaire's warning not to press him. Carmine throws his door open and storms around the car. I tuck my face into the crook of my arm, bracing for what's to come. He reaches in, yanks me out by the forearm, and shuts the door. I tried to peel his fingers off my arm, but his grip was too tight. He releases and shoves me toward the man all at once. They exchange handshakes, and Carmine gets back in the car and drives away, leaving me with this stranger.

I back away from the man and remove my heels. He shakes his head, but I do what my instincts tell me to do.

Run.

Chapter Twenty-Six
Hungry

The flat surface aids in my escape as I sprint over the pristine landscape. In the distance, a break in the fence gives me hope that I may make it.

I'm wrong.

The man tackles my legs from behind, and we fall to the grass. Stabbing pain pierces through my center as though the accident is happening again. The man lifts the opening in my dress and gawks at the bruising across my side as I scream.

My feet kick as he moves off me, and one of my heels nails him in the groin. He tips over and lands in a heap beside me.

"I'm not trying to hurt you." He groans in agony.

Grass curls into my fist as I fight against the agonizing fire on my side. I push myself onto my palms and knees and crawl toward the opening. The man forces himself upright and towers above me.

"Please, Mia. I only wish to speak with you over a meal."

"What?"

"Carmine and I have an agreement. I will provide some information to him if I can sit and have lunch with you. That's all."

"What information?"

"I'm sorry. I can't discuss it." The man lowers his palm to me. "Come."

My fingers refuse to let go of the green swords wrapped around them. Fear holds me hostage, and I brace for a painful reprimand for not following orders. It never came. Instead, the man takes out his phone and asks the person on the other line to meet us on the lawn.

He sits next to me, extends his limbs, and crosses them at the ankles.

"Beautiful day for a picnic. Don't you think?"

A golf cart rolls toward us as I release the grass and sit upright. A red-haired woman wearing an apron and a man dressed like a butler exit. They unload a checkered blanket and shake it out. Two pillows rest opposite each other, and a plate is in front of each.

The woman offers me her hand, helps me to my pillow, and drops a fabric napkin on my lap. The butler rests an oversized basket in the center of the square. They nod to us and drive away.

"Who are you?" I ask as he opens the wicker.

"My name is Marco."

"Why am I here?"

"We are having a picnic." He grins as he places a bundle of seedless green grapes on my dinnerware. "Hungry?"

"Yes, but why me?"

"Well, Mia, I, like Carmine, am single. He claimed you as his own, but nothing is set in stone. He ordered me to stay away from you, but recent events brought him to me for some information. So, I agreed to help under one condition."

"Lunch with me."

"Correct."

Marco removes a grape from the vine and holds it before my lips. I hesitated at first, then accepted his offer.

This is my chance to turn them on each other. No one is around, so I shift my pillow, and a hint of my cheek peeks out from under my dress. Carmine made a mistake by not letting me wear underwear.

A smile tugs at the corner of Marco's mouth. He reaches into the basket and pulls out a bottle of wine and two glasses. The cork pops, and a wisp of smoke floats into the air.

Marco pours me a quarter of a glass, and I raise my brow. He fills it higher and laughs through his perfect nose.

"Did Carmine do that to your ribs?"

"No. A car accident."

"The one where Nick hit a tree, and someone shot him?"

"Yes," I answer, growing uncomfortable.

"Mia, Carmine does not tolerate withholding information from him."

A small orange stain on the blanket held my attention, as I refuse to make eye contact. My fingers roll the material between them. A breeze sends his woodsy scent to my side. I inhale it and think about Tony. He's coming. I need to stall.

Marco's palm rests on my calf. "You should've told him the truth when he asked."

"I'm afraid."

"Who are you more scared of, Carmine or the man who killed his son?"

"Both."

"No, Mia. Nicoli's killer spared you twice, once in the car and once in the dressing room. Each time, he lets you live. Why?"

"I'm not sure."

"Liar," he hisses as he grips my leg hard.

My breaths quicken as his demeanor changes from calm and collected, to fierce and unpredictable.

"You're breaking an important rule, Mia. Always tell the truth."

"These are not my rules, and I do not belong here!" I screamed in his face.

"Carmine said you are a stubborn girl." He snatches my hair and wraps his hand around it. "I can't help you unless you help me."

"With what?"

"The truth!" Marco spits as he shouts in frustration.

A car squeals in our direction. Carmine is coming back, and I've run out of time. The car door opens, and Carmine exits, rolling up his sleeves. A passenger passes him an envelope through the window.

Marco stands and gazes down at me. "I can't help you now. No one can." He turns his back to me and walks toward the house.

I scurry to my feet and throw my arms in front of my face as Carmine reaches for me. The force of his shaking disorients me as my brain rattles inside my skull.

"Sit down." He orders, forcing me to the earth.

Images float around me as he dumps the contents of the packet on my head. Tony's face surrounds me. I picked up a picture from outside Stevie's bar. Tony is loading me into my car.

"Who is he?" Carmine asks as he blocks the sun with his body.

I shrug my shoulders and glance at a bee landing on a flower.

"Liar," he yells, pulling Tony's hat from his back pocket and striking me in the face with it. "My men found this at your house. A friend of Marcos tested his hair. It belongs to Antonius Scalucci. The man you call Tony."

"Please, Carmine, you don't understand."

He squats down before me and grabs my face. "What don't I understand?"

"Tony stalked me. He followed me wherever I went and left messages on my phone."

"Did he?"

"Yes." I cry.

"Do you know why?"

"No."

"He used you for bait to draw out my son. You are a stupid girl. All the things he did to you were meant to scare you into calling Nicoli to save you. Tony tried to draw him out. It didn't work, so Tony called one of my son's men and gave them your location. Nicoli loved you, and Tony used that love to murder him." Carmine shouts as he yanks me to my feet. "He's dead because of you."

"No. Why would he?"

"Because you witnessed Nicoli kill his brother and left him because of it."

"The man Nick killed in the alley was Tony's brother?"

"This whole fiasco is about revenge, and you, willing or not, are a part of it."

"I didn't know, Carmine. You must believe me." I sob.

"I do, but I don't believe he never told you his name. Am I right?"

"Only his first name," I admit.

"And yet you held that from me."

"Yes."

Carmine pulls me close to him and stares into my eyes. "Did you have sex with him? Did you sleep with my son's killer? I saw the surveillance from the hotel when Nicoli came to retrieve you. Tony exited your room, adjusting himself within thirty minutes of Nicoli's arrival. You fucked him, didn't you?"

Silence isn't an answer, but Carmine needs no reply. He slaps me across the face, knocking me to the ground.

"Answer me, whore!"

His fists coil as he screams at a dark cloud hovering over us. A drop of water splatters on my forehead and joins the tears on my face.

"Did you?" He shouts.

"Yes."

Carmine grabs the hair on both sides of his head, and the blood-curdling scream that followed came straight out of my worst nightmare.

"Mia, on your feet, now." His voice is suddenly calm.

I am slow to stand, irritating him. He takes hold of the twisted fabric on my chest and yanks me to the vehicle.

"I warned you what would happen if you lied to me. I gave you every opportunity to tell me everything, to tell me the truth, but you still protected him."

I opened my mouth to speak, and he hit me on the side of the head, taking my hearing. Rain bursts from the clouds muddying the soil under me. The falling droplets flood the yard with ponds of liquid.

Carmine grasps my head, forces it over a deep puddle, and plunges it inside.

I gasp for air every time he pulls me back out. My fingers dig into the mud as I try and keep him from doing it again, to no avail.

Again and again, he sticks my head beneath the dark surface. Each time is longer than the last. White specks of light dot my vision, and dizziness zaps my strength.

He's winning. So, I stopped fighting and let him drown me.

Chapter Twenty-Seven
Breathe

No light is visible in this dark place, as people say. There is no one waiting for me on the other side. God is not here to receive me, nor am I someplace better. I wander around for a few seconds before someone screams my name in the distance.

At first, I paid little mind to it. But it grew louder and louder. The man's voice echoes in the shadows far above me. If I remain here, would anyone miss me? Would the screaming cease with time? I wish my mother were here. The decision would be easier. I would take her hand, and she would lead me to the beyond or wherever this place goes.

'Mia…' The voice booms from somewhere unknown.

It ricochets around the empty space like stereo sound in a movie theater. My body falls away from the darkness, and a bright light shimmers like the North Star over my weightless frame. I float toward it, hoping it is the entrance to the gates of heaven.

Water chokes from my airway as Carmine ceases CPR. Death would've been easier. Anything is better than knowing the man in front of me who took my life also saved it. This isn't heaven. Not even close. I arrived right back where I started…in hell.

Marco hovers over his shoulder, shielding us with his jacket from the raging storm. His eyes glance up at the sky as he thanks the lord above.

Carmine pulls me to his chest. His heavy breaths warm my chilled scalp. Though his embrace is sincere, it isn't because he cares or loves me. More like, if I am dead, he has no one to blame, take his out pain on, or a body to carry his child. He brought me to arm's length and parted his lips to speak, but nothing came out.

I waited for an apology, but it never came. He picks me up and carries me inside Marco's. Carmine lays me on a guest bed, covers my shivering body with a blanket, and leaves the room with Marco.

The bedroom is black, white, and red. The ruby curtains add a dash of color to the ink walls. The comforter is bright white with imprinted floral images sewn in. Chattering from my teeth produces the only sound in the room. A television sits above an unlit fireplace.

The vase beside me holds a bouquet of colorful lilies. A woman in a green polka-dotted summer dress dances around a flowered bush with several children holding hands. I hum 'Ring Around the Rosie' to myself. I'm at the 'falling down' part when Marco enters the room holding a tray.

He stands beside me, sets the tray down, and fluffs the pillow under my head. His face is pale in comparison to when we first met. Perhaps he had never seen someone die and come back to life before. Marco places a broth-filled spoon before my lips, but I reject it. I'd rather be cold and starving than accept his guilt gumbo.

"What are you doing?" Carmine asks, entering the room.

"She's freezing. I warmed up some soup." Marco says, resting the utensil back in the bowl. "She won't take it. I think she's in shock."

"Doesn't matter. We aren't staying," Carmine scoffs as he tosses the blanket away from me. "The storm is over."

The cold draft sends chills across my naked flesh as Carmine reaches under me and lifts me off the bed. The fight in me returns, and he drops me when I struggle in his arms.

My hands hit crooked as I crashed to the floor, dislocating both my thumbs. They jump right back into place but are now useless, painful appendages. Carmine seizes me by the upper arm and drags my screaming, flailing body outside with Marco in tow.

He launches me into the side of his waiting vehicle, striking my head on the framework and cutting it open—the concrete ground tearing into my knees. Blood drips onto the white driveway as I fold into a fetal position.

"Carmine is this necessary," Marco says, reaching for me.

"Necessary? She slept with the man responsible for killing my son and lied to me about knowing him. Mia has broken several rules. No level of pain or cruelty is enough."

"Mia, stand up. I have an important dinner this evening," Carmine says as he throws the car door aside.

My elbow rests on the seat as I take a deep breath and prepare to force myself inside. Carmine doesn't wish to wait. He places both hands on my buttocks and stuffs me in. I retreat as far away from him as I can. The door slams, and we drive away from Marco's house.

The silent ride to his mansion made me wish he didn't save my life. Tension, rage, and pain emanate from his body like solar rays scorching my skin. Holding my hands does little to steady their shaking. My thumbs are throbbing, and I rub them softly.

The gates of the property ground open, allowing us to enter. Up ahead, Blaire and two armed men stand outside, waiting for us. When the door opens, Carmine walks away with the guards.

"Poor girl," Blaire says, leaning in. "It's okay. Come to me."

I flinched away from her and held the door. Rain on the glass distorts Carmine and his men's appearance as they talk on the lawn. Blaire appears in my field of vision on my side of the car, and she lets herself in. She wraps a sweater around my shoulders, and I lean my sopping, frozen frame into her. Carmine approaches us as she helps me into the house. I thought he might follow, but instead, he stepped into his office without looking in our direction.

As we pass a mirror in the hall, I stop. The person in the reflection is unrecognizable. A deep cut on my head bleeds at the hairline, and bruises dot every visible inch of skin. My knees are brush burned and red, and the bases of my thumbs on my palms are purple from trauma. The hair on my head is a jumbled mess of tangled strands.

"Mia, this way."

Blaire tries to pull me away, but I plant my feet. There is something in my eyes that is different. Emptiness. That's what it is. There is nothing there. I left it behind in the lonely darkness of death. I touch my face to see if I am real as Blaire tugs at me a second time, this time with more force.

"Mia, please," she begs as I stiffen my body.

When I turn to her, I see the disparity in her eyes. She's afraid for me, more than I am for myself. Her eyes glance over my shoulder, scanning for Carmine. I give in and let her shift my body to face the hall.

I didn't bother asking her where we were going. It doesn't matter anymore. My sole purpose now is to be Carmine's punching bag. After his meal, I expect more punishment for my lies and betrayal. I'm no one to him. Just a stupid girl whom he believes played a part in his son's death. To him, I am a damaged shell—an empty, frail, lifeless object. Once I provide Carmine with a son, he will no doubt toss me into the ocean.

Tony said he would come for me, but it won't be in time. Carmine already killed me once. No one would have saved me if he hadn't done it himself. I can't count on Tony.

If I survive what happens next, tomorrow I can devise a plan. For now, I must take what Carmine thinks I deserve. Blaire rests her hand on my upper back and steers me away from the stranger in the mirror.

Chapter Twenty-Eight
Time

Blaire turns the faucet on and pours a scented bubble bath into the tub. Although her intentions are sincere, they won't improve my mood. Life's a bitch, and hormones wait for no one.

Liquid escapes my body and ventures down my inner thigh. Blood rolls over the inside of my foot and lands on the white tile.

Blaire cringes, reaches into the suds, and pulls the plug.

A shower doesn't exist in this bathroom, only a handheld attachment. I made no motion to move as Blaire grabs her supplies and leaves the room.

My cycle is early, and this isn't good. It's my 'off month.' That's what I call it. Every other period is hell. I'm moody, miserable, and suffer from severe cramps.

"I've got some medicine for you," Blaire says, reentering the room. "It's a diuretic."

She drops two blue pills in my palm and hands me a glass of water. The drink crashes to the floor as my right thumb does not supply enough strength to hold it. Blaire shakes her head, leaves the room, and returns with another beverage. This time she holds it for me. I gulp the medication down like a dehydrated desert walker who has just found water. Perhaps that is where I am, in the desert, and this is all a mirage. A clot escapes from my center and plops on the floor.

They're coming. The twisting, gut-wrenching, agonizing contractions have arrived. My womb hates me. I grip my abdomen and double over.

"Mia, you need a hot shower. The heat helps."

She leads me by the arm out of the room, leaving a trail of blood behind us. After a short trip, we arrive at a guest bedroom with a full walk-in shower and glass walls around it. I shuffle in and drop to my knees. Blaire steps over to a stone wall and cranks the water on.

Rain falls from a system hanging from the ceiling, encapsulating me. She leans into the enclosed space, unzips the dress from my hunched back, and slips it to my waist. I pull myself apart long enough to take the outfit off.

A knife rotates inside, making me cry out. Crimson particles swirl down the drain as water pelts my naked flesh. A heavy hand strokes my hair. The last person I expected sympathy from was Carmine. Perhaps the only pain that's acceptable is the kind he causes. I hyperventilate as another round of contractions folds me further into myself.

Carmine removes his clothes and climbs in beside me. He takes my head off the white porcelain and rests it on his bare leg.

"My wife suffered, much like you are now. We would come in here until the heat and medicine reduced her cramping to a tolerable level."

He's doing this for her, not for me. She isn't here, but our similarities make it hard for him to be cruel to me during this difficult time. When he closes his eyes, I imagine he pictures her on the shower floor instead of me.

Carmine runs his pointer along a four-inch blemish on my lower right abdomen. "What's the story here?"

"Appendix."

"You and my wife have a lot in common. Books, heavy periods, strong spirit, and now an appendectomy scar." His last words stagger from his lips.

The loss of his spouse is still fresh and weighs on his heart. The positive is it's keeping me alive. But at what cost? He wants to marry me and have children, not necessarily in that order.

"Oh God," I cry out, gripping my pressurized pelvis.

Carmine knocks on the steamy glass wall, and Blaire appears in the doorway. "She needs something stronger."

"Yes, sir."

A few seconds later, Blaire passes a round white pill to Carmine. He places it before my lips. I don't question its ingredients as I take it into my mouth and sip the water he offers me. His right palm rubs my stomach in a soft circle while his left pets my head. Euphoria spreads throughout my system after several minutes, and I can sit up for the first time in hours.

"They're gone," I announce.

"Good," Carmine says as he takes my face.

My breath quickens as he pulls my head to him and kisses me. I move away from him as his mouth readies for another kiss.

"Carmine, what did you give me?" I say, keeping my outstretched arm between us.

"Do you feel better?"

"Yes, but…"

"No buts." Carmine orders, cutting me off and pushing my forearm down. "I took your pain away. The least you can do is give me something in return."

I'd rather be in pain than give him anything. If I knew beforehand, I would have rejected his remedy.

Before I have a chance to react, his palm cups my neck, and yanks my face to his. He shoves his tongue into my mouth violently.

I push him back as I struggle to a standing position, wipe my lips, and shove the door aside. "No."

My toes curl into the plush mat outside the partition when I exit the enclosure. I grab a peach towel and use my working fingers to wrap it around me loosely. Blaire left a satin nightgown, maxi pad, and underwear on a bench by the toilet. Tampons are what I use, but this is all they have.

"Mia?" Carmine speaks through the bathroom door.

"Just a minute." I can't even use the toilet in peace.

The floor creaks on the other side of the door. He's waiting for me. I have a feeling if I stay in here, he will stand there for hours or break the door down and drag me out. Why delay the inevitable? I flush, wash my hands, and open the door.

Carmine is standing naked in front of me. His fifth limb dangles between his legs. My cheeks redden as I try not to stare.

"Blaire made the bed in here for us."

"Us?"

"Yes. Mia."

"Don't you have a dinner party or something tonight?"

"I canceled when Blaire advised me of your situation."

"You still need to eat."

"And so do you," Carmine smiles, reaching for my hand.

I glare at it. How can he think I'm comfortable lying next to him after he killed me? Does he think we are friends now because he comforted me and supplied pain relief? I don't want his sympathy or his pills. I want my freedom.

A sharp, hot poker, drives its way into my lower abdomen, doubling me over. Carmine seizes me by the elbow and leads me to the side of the bed.

He moves the comforter aside, adjusts the pillows, and helps me in. My eyes follow him as he strolls around to his side, and crawls in beside me. Before covering me up, he retrieves a heated water bottle from the side table and rests it on my stomach.

"Blaire!" Carmine hollers at the door as he covers me up making me jump.

She enters with a massive tray, sets it on the side table, and removes the lids from the food. A knife sits on the side of one plate, waiting for use. I stared at her with overly wide eyes trying to get her attention. If she would just hand it to me, I could use it as a weapon. Instead, she stoops down, reaches under the bed, and pulls out two folding lap tables. Each of us receives a metallic circular platter with bacon-wrapped filet mignon, mashed potatoes, and a dinner roll.

After getting us a glass of ice water, Blaire passes a remote control to Carmine. A skunky smell drifts from her fingers as she removes the wet bandage from my head and replaces it with a dry one. We make brief eye contact as she squeezes my arm and sighs. Her eyes are glossy, as though she's been crying.

"That'll be all, Blaire," Carmine orders as he switches the television on and starts eating.

I sit motionless, not eating and not understanding. How can this man go from killing me one day to treating me as though we are in a relationship the next? Inside my head, I wonder if he is insane.

Carmine reaches over to my tray, cuts a piece of steak, and hovers it in front of my face.

I hesitate to open my mouth, and he presses it against my tender lips. "Open, now," he insists with dark, angry eyes. Normal Carmine has returned.

The morsel enters my mouth. Carmine smiles when I raise my brow and stab the next piece on my own. Holding the fork between my pointer and middle finger while using my ring finger for support resembled a toddler learning how to use utensils for the first time. It does the job despite how silly it looks. I scarf down one delicious piece after another. My voracious appetite devours it all within minutes. I haven't had a proper meal since I arrived at the mansion, and it shows. Juices drip down my chin, and I swipe them with the back of my hand. I gaze down at Carmine's half-eaten part. I'm full, but my brain wants more.

Carmine cuts a small piece away, picks it up with two fingers, and turns to me.

"Want more?"

"Yes," I say softly.

He places the beef between his lips and leans toward me. I lean back. *Gross.* He grabs my arms, draws me to him, and shoves the bite and his tongue into my mouth. His fingers grip my chin as he moves my jaw up and down. I yank my head away and finish chewing on my own. Once I swallow, I stare straight ahead, ignoring him. I sense his eyes on me as he takes another piece and places it in his mouth. He's waiting for me to turn to him, but I hold my ground and continue watching television.

The television clicks off and the mattress shifts up as Carmine stands. He strolls to my side of the bed, and I continue to gaze at the black screen across the room. In my peripheral vision, he bends his bare frame beside me. The air from his nose moves the fine hairs of my cheekbone. When he turns my face to him, I keep my eyes facing the front. He gives my head a forceful shake, and I turn my attention to him. His fingers slide to the back of my scalp, giving me goosebumps as he plunges the next bite into my mouth. As he moves his head away, he keeps his eyes fixed on mine. He's waiting for me to chew and swallow, determined to keep using his tongue as my utensil. I open my mouth and wait to accept my next bite like a starving child.

This side of him is safe. He's using meat as foreplay, which is weird but not physically painful. I may never eat filet again after I escape this place, or beef, for that matter. I will stick to poultry. If tomorrow night this fiasco continues with a stuffing-filled chicken breast, I may become a vegan. Carmine clears his throat, waiting for me to accept more. I comply and open as he continues feeding me like a baby bird. He chuckles and bites his lip after stuffing the last piece inside me. His eyes are pinpoint and glossy. He's on something. There is no other explanation for his odd behavior.

For now, I will play Jekyll's twisted game, but I will keep my guard up, for Hyde waits beneath the surface.

Chapter Twenty-Nine
Family

Sleeping with the enemy isn't so bad when you're on drugs. My physical and mental status is under the influence of some stellar narcotics. Blaire brought me another pill in the middle of the night when the earlier one wore off. I can't stop thinking about how I feel. *Numb*. It's starting to wear off, and I want another.

Now I realize why people become addicted. The problem is, when the 'high' wears off, the pain returns, physically, and mentally.

Last night after Carmine fed me like a bird, he turned me to my side and gave me a back massage. I cringed with every press of his palm into my painful muscles. He is mindful not to touch my bruised ribs. I don't know why. As soon as I piss him off, he will crush them with torturous pressure. When he finished moisturizing my skin, he handed me a couple of pills and watched me take them.

I don't remember falling asleep. One minute I stared at a flaw in the wallpaper across from me, and the next, the sun was shining on my face through a window. If it weren't for my period and Carmine, I would stay in bed all day. Both are uncomfortable, and neither one is giving up until they're finished with me.

Carmine holds me against his bare frame. I carefully removed his arm and slipped out of bed. The guest bathroom has sanitary supplies, an extra change of clothes, and medicine to carry me for a few days. Not the good kind. *Bummer*.

Today is terrible, but nothing compared to yesterday. Stress feeds my cycle like a catalyst, zapping my strength. An unexpected tear drops on the shiny marble surface—the pain

inside fights to exit, swelling my abdomen beyond its natural
ability.

If the Grim Reaper stood before me and led me to an early
grave, I wouldn't object. Instead, Carmine stands in the
doorway naked, watching me.

"Take another pill."

Oh, sure. Take another pill so my guard can be down, and
you can play more childish games with me. No, thank you, Mr.
Ed.

"I'm fine," I say, trying not to gawk at his third leg. "Would
it kill you to put on pants?"

"No," Carmine says, passing me a glass of water and
medicine. "Don't be stubborn."

I snatch them out of his palm and gulp the room-temperature
liquid. The tablet scrapes down my throat and lands in my
vacant stomach. My palms are dark purple now as the full
extent of the bilateral dislocation reveals itself. The bruising
wraps from halfway between my pointer and thumb base,
through the center of my palm, and down to my wrist. Carmine
makes no move to leave as I grab toilet paper, wrap a beehive
around my hand, and swipe the red sludge between my legs.

Carmine flushes for me as I pull my panties into place.

"That's a lot of blood. Blaire can pick up some iron this
afternoon."

"No. It makes me sick."

"Suit yourself," Carmine sighs, walking away as I wash my
hands.

Blaire is in the guest bedroom when I come into the room.
She is stripping the bed and tossing the soiled sheets into a pile
on the floor. When I snuck away this morning, I didn't see the
stains.

"Sorry, Blaire," I say, picking up the linens. "Let me help
you."

"Don't be silly. It happens. After you put on more clothes,
meet me in the kitchen. I'm making breakfast."

Blaire smiles with her eyes as she takes the bundle of
laundry from me. I pull on baby blue stretch waist shorts and

switch my gown for a black t-shirt. When I enter the kitchen, Carmine is still clothesless as he hangs an appointment calendar on the wall by the refrigerator.

A bird visits a feeder outside a picture window, and I focus on it as it pecks at the various seeds. Footsteps approach me, but I pretend not to notice. Carmine makes me stand and forces me onto his lap. I squirm as he hardens under my shorts and kisses my neck.

"I can't wait until my son is inside you," Carmine whispers as he touches my stomach. "He will be a strong and handsome leader. Just like his father and Nicoli."

"And what if I have a girl first? Will you let her be in a position of power?"

"You can teach your daughter whatever you like, but women rarely run the family," Carmine says as he squeezes my waist. "I won't stop until we have a son. You can take care of the rest."

My son. Your daughter.

In other words, he will pay no mind to the girls, only his son. I can see it now, I will have an army of girls, and since they are mine, I will train them to torment him to death. It will be the ultimate punishment for not treating us as equals.

"What are you grinning about?" Carmine asks.

I didn't realize I was. "Women can be just as ruthless as men, you know?"

One of his men enters, interrupting our conversation.

"Sir, Marco is on the line."

Carmine holds me from behind and breathes a heavy, hot breath through my top. "Coming."

He lifts me off him and sets me on the cushioned chair. His soldiers see him wandering around the house nude all the time, but I find it a bit much.

I remove the calendar from the wall when he leaves the room. The word 'ovulation window' stretches across a ten-day stretch in bold letters. Carmine is planning our pregnancy. Although he said he wouldn't force me, he did say he expected a 'yes' when the time came.

The month-to-month drops to the floor. Blaire reaches in front of my motionless frame. She raises it to her face and reads what Carmine wrote.

"Everything is fine. Don't worry," she says, hanging it back up.

I weep on her shoulder when she draws me into her warm embrace. Blaire combs my hair with her fingertips and murmurs, "Come with me, sweet girl."

Blaire releases me and walks toward the sunroom. Once inside, she shuts the door and pats the seats of the brown leather couch. My bare thighs sweat as I wait for her to collect her thoughts.

"Nicoli was my grandson."

The confession blurts out of her mouth as though some internal force launched it from her body. Her fingers fumble against her lips as she holds back her emotions. I'm too shocked to respond, so I listen.

"I was pregnant when Carmine's parents hired me as his nanny. They let me stay despite my condition when I found out. I delivered Sophie right in this room on their Persian rug. I thought for sure they'd fire me. But instead, they welcomed us. As it turns out, Carmine and Sophie shared a tight bond. So, as soon as Sophie turned eighteen, they got married. Nine months later, Sophie gave birth to Nicoli. Life used to be simple. Nothing like now."

"I wonder why he never told me."

"Well, it may not be a huge deal to most, but when you are second in command, having a grandmother who's a housekeeper doesn't scream our family is powerful."

I fiddle with my fingertips in my lap, wondering if she blames me for Nick's murder as Carmine does. I would.

"You must hate me," I sob.

"Of course not. Nicoli loved you. His death is not on your hands. It's on Carmine's. He's the one who ordered Nicoli to kill the man you left him over. I tried to tell him it didn't make sense, but he wouldn't listen. How can you retrieve money from a person when they're dead? Carmine always kept a strong hold on Nicoli. Years ago, Nicoli was so sweet and caring about everything and everyone, despite his behavior problems. When other families and friends took advantage of his kind nature, Carmine came down on him hard. He feared Nicoli's upbringing was soft. Before too long, Nick became someone I didn't recognize. When Sophie tried to intervene and express how she felt to Carmine, they had the worst argument I have ever heard. Sophie didn't think I knew he hit her that night, but I could see it in her eyes. He hurt her. A mother always knows. They had their spats here and there as all couples do but he's never hurt her up until that point. When it came to Nicoli's upbringing, Carmine drew a line in the sand. No one, not even Sophie, was going to tell him how to raise his son. The more Carmine dug into Nicoli, the further he withdrew from us. Sophie and I were heartbroken. When he met you, you brought out the boy we used to know. Every time he visited you, he returned a different person. You brought our Nicoli back to us. At least, a small part of him anyway."

"Blaire, I don't want to be here," I cry. "Carmine isn't who I want to marry, let alone have children with."

"Listen to me, Mia. A storm is coming. Perhaps not today, but soon. All we need to do is hang on a little longer."

"What do you mean?"

"It's better for you to remain in the dark. Knowing too much can be dangerous."

"I'm already in danger," I grimace.

"Mia, in order for this plan to work, you need to get your hands dirty as well."

"What plan?"

"What I'm about to ask you may cause you harm or worse. But if it works, we can be free from this family," Blaire says as she turns her body away from the camera in the corner.

"I'll do anything to be free of this hell."

"Seduce Marco."

"Well, maybe not that."

"Mia, it is the only way. I know his intentions are the same as Carmine's, but he's not as ruthless or as observant. Marco will be easier to manipulate."

"Manipulate how?"

"Carmine is too smart to fall for any tricks. He would see right through you. His intuition is extremely high. You couldn't lure him to bed if you tried, despite how much he wants it. If Marco believes that you are interested and he knows Carmine is the only thing standing in the way of being with you, he will take care of him. We wouldn't need to lift a finger."

"But what about after? I don't want to be stuck with Marco either."

"You let me worry about that."

Chapter Thirty
The Calm Before

I played Blaire's plan in my head many times throughout the day.

Creating a divide between Marco and Carmine is the only chance I have. The downside is Marco will want something in return if he kills Carmine because of me. Perhaps we can work out a deal. I could offer him the money Nick left me in his will. Who wouldn't want an extra few million dollars, right? It would suck for me, but I'd rather be poor and free than rich and miserable.

Blaire has a plan of her own as well but refuses to share it with me. There is one problem I haven't figured out. Carmine is keeping Marco away from me. The picnic was a one-time arrangement in exchange for information on Tony.

Blaire said not to worry, and that it's being 'handled,' but she never said how.

Carmine joins me in the sunroom, taking a seat across from me. The silky red pants he's put on shine in the morning sun. He's still not wearing underwear, but something is better than nothing.

I continue reading, pretending to be oblivious to his presence. My stomach shakes as he leans forward in his chair and tilts his head. His palms slide against each other as if he's contemplating using them.

The last few paragraphs I've read are a blur, and I reread them. Focusing is difficult when someone gives you a death stare from across the room.

"Mia, ignoring me isn't going to make me go away. It's just pissing me off," his stern voice proclaims.

I rest my book on the coffee table, face down and open. Carmine's eyes burn holes through me as he approaches and sits beside me. I gaze out at the garden and focus on a perfect rose bloom. My head flies back as Carmine grabs my hair, yanking me to him.

"Don't push me. I can have anyone. Impregnate anyone. Have a child with anyone. You are insignificant to me, but you meant something to my son. So don't think you are indispensable."

He tosses my head away from him, cracking my neck. It wasn't intentional, but my eyes turned dark as I spilled a fact of my own.

"Dispense of me then. Because I'd rather be dead than have a baby with y…."

The last word didn't escape my lips as Carmine struck me with his fist. Swelling took the sight from my left eye as I land hard on the rug. The hit knocked all my senses out of me at once. Hyde has returned.

Carmine turns me onto my back and sits on my abdomen. "The only part of you I need is from this point down," he says, touching my belly button. "The rest is fair game."

His face comes within an inch of mine as he wedges his lower half between my legs—hints of bacon float from his mouth as he speaks.

"I could take you right here and now." Carmine grinds his rolling pin into my pelvis. "But I chose to wait. Choose to give you time to adjust to your new life. Time for you to accept the inevitable."

"Never," I chuckle, antagonizing him.

Like Nick, Carmine stands and drags me by the hair out of the room. Blaire reaches for me as we pass the doorway she is standing in. I see her hustle into the office and shut the door through my one-functioning eye.

Carmine lifts me off the floor and throws me onto an unfamiliar mattress. Handcuffs wrap around my wrists, one then the other, pinching my skin. One of my heels hits him in the chest. His palm grapples my thigh and squeezes it into submission as I scream. He slides the drawer beside us open and removes a pair of scissors. I buck on the bed, trying to get away from him.

"Hold still," Carmine orders as he grips my throat.

I stop moving as the blade of the shear travels between my breasts down to my waist. Carmine cuts my shirt up its center and yanks it from behind my back. Then he does the same with my shorts. I hold my breath as he reaches for my underwear.

A sharp knock at the door stops everything. Carmine huffs through his nostrils and dismounts me to answer, slamming the door behind him. I hyperventilate alone on this blanketless bed and wonder what his plans for me are.

Someone is shouting inaudible words in the hallway. The sound of multiple gunshots comes from outside. No matter how much I thrashed about, I couldn't free myself. A loud boom rocks the mansion, vibrating the chandelier above me. A glass on the stand shatters to the floor. Smoke billows beneath the door, choking me with its density.

The bedroom door whips open, and Blaire pauses. "Time to go," she announces, removing a bobby pin from her tight grey bun.

"What's going on?"

"Not now, Mia," she coughs.

Blaire stuffs the V-shaped metal tip into the keyhole of the cuffs and wiggles them until they unlock. She grabs a sweatshirt from the closet by the door and throws it at me. I stuff myself into it as we enter the smoke-filled hallway. Carmine and two of his men join us as Blaire pulls my uncooperative body behind her. Carmine pushes a panel in the walkway, and a secret exit opens. We descended a small staircase that leads to an underground garage.

The dizziness from having my bell rung makes walking fast and in a straight line impossible. Only being able to see out of one eye is not helping either. Carmine takes me from Blaire when I almost fall and carries me the rest of the way.

He loads me into a black four-door sedan. I'm placed in the middle of the back seat, and Blaire and Carmine each take a side. My body falls over and lands on Carmine's shoulder. I try and force myself the other way, but my head is heavy, so I leave it there. Carmine holds me steady as the driver slams on the gas and launches the car out of the underground parking garage.

The mansion is on fire when I slide my face against the leather and peer behind us. Tony. It has to be. He has come for me. A smile tugs at the corner of my mouth as I picture myself sitting in a camp chair in front of the flames. I take an oversized marshmallow, press it onto a long wooden skewer, and eat smores as Carmine's family home burns.

Carmine peers over his shoulder, and then down at my smiling expression. I have no time to react. No time to brace myself for what's coming. Blaire grabs Carmine's hands and tries to stop him from shaking me. If I were a baby, I would be dead already.

He shrieks in my face, "Do you think this is funny?"

My face stings as a harsh slap strikes it. But it doesn't stop me, and my defiant grin returns.

"Stubborn girl," Carmine hisses as he taps the driver.

We pull over in a wooded area. Carmine opens the door and pulls me out of the car. Blaire moves to our side to exit as well, but Carmine slams the car door in her face. The lock clicks as the driver locks her in, and me out.

Gravel digs into my knees as Carmine forces me to the ground. He pulls out his gun and points it at me. I close my eyes when he rests the barrel on my forehead. The metallic weapon glides down the bridge of my nose and stops on my quivering lips.

"This would be easy if I didn't need you."

Carmine tucks the gun back into his waistband and exhales as he wipes his mouth with the palm of his hand. His hands rest on his hips as his weight shifts from one foot to the other.

"Look at me, Mia."

I keep my head down.

"Look at me!" He screams.

I tilt my head and catch a glimpse of the blue sky right before Carmine's open hand smacks me across the lips, splitting them open. Blood drools from my mouth onto my sweatshirt. I lift my head up high, and smile a blood-stained, toothy smile, at him. It earns me another strike, splitting my lips further.

The window beside me rolls down, and Blaire sticks her head out. "Carmine, please, stop."

He removes a white handkerchief from his inside pocket, wipes the blood from his hands, then uses his foot to kick me over. My head strikes the road when I land. Blaire makes eye contact with me and shakes her head. She wants me to stop pushing him, testing him, antagonizing him.

For now, he has won, but only because I have lost the strength to take any more blows. Tomorrow is another day, and we can pick up where we left off then. I won't stop fighting him. Not now. Not ever. Even if it kills me.

Chapter Thirty-One
Tension

As we travel up a tree-lined hill, I realize we are heading to Marco's. The last time I came here, Carmine drowned me in a puddle.

I grip Blaire's hand as the memory comes rushing back. My throat closes as we round the corner, and Marco's chalet appears. No air is coming or going from me. Oxygen sticks in my windpipe as my face turns red.

"Mia, breathe," Blaire says, turning my face to hers. "In through your nose, out through your mouth."

The closer the car came to the house, the faster my breaths became. When the vehicle rolls to a stop, everyone exits except for me. I pick at the dried blister on my finger and fixate my eyes on the carpet.

Blaire leans in and whispers, "Remember the plan."

I nod to her and take the hand she offers me. Carmine glares at me as Blaire helps me inside. The shaking has turned violent, and I can't control it. My legs buckle, and I fall inside Marco's threshold.

Marco runs to me, but Carmine raises his hand. "She's fine." He says, lifting me by the arm.

With Marco on his heels, Carmine pulls my staggering body to the guest bedroom. "Carmine, what happened to her face? Does she need a doctor? She could have a concussion."

"No one leaves. That's the rule. Mia broke it, and she is getting punished," he hisses through clenching teeth as he tosses me on the bed.

"Don't you think she's had enough? You already killed her once," Marco reminds him.

"Mia's had enough when I say she has, and not a minute before," Carmine yells, startling me.

Marco sighs through his nose as Carmine pushes past him into the hallway. He stands at the end of the bed and squeezes its wooden footboard.

"The doctor is visiting my father for his yearly check-up this afternoon. She plans to stay a few days. I'll ask her to come see you as well," Marco says as his voice trails off and he leaves the room.

The door clicks as he or someone else locks it from the outside. My bruised legs slip under the white Egyptian cotton sheets, and I pass out.

In my dreams, I am safe. I wade through the shallow waves of the ocean and smile as little fish nibble at my toes. The sun warms my battered skin and heals my damaged soul. In the distance, sitting on the shore is a man with a blurry face waving at me. Peace envelopes me as I sink into the deep water and let it wash my cares away.

But this is just…

A dream…?

A wish…?

A prayer answered…?

My eyelids flicker open and back to reality.

No.

It's a lie…plain and simple. I have no future if I can't find a way out of this life.

Red stains dot the pillow beneath my head. The covers fall away as I push myself upright and tiptoe to the restroom. The floor is chilly under my bare feet, but the seat is warm when I sit down. An orange light, with squiggly lines floating above the image of a toilet, flashes in the mirror's reflection to my right. Heated throne. How unnecessary. It is a cool feature, but I am sure it costs more than it's worth.

My eyes widen at the sight of myself in the mirror. Various shades of purple and green cover my face in multiple locations. My lips appear as though I had too much filler injected into them.

The bleeding from my body has slowed to normal levels, but the pain remains. Sudden yelling jerks my half-awake frame.

The voices become louder and come from the other side of the door.

Marco, Carmine, and a tall, tan woman with long black hair and model cheekbones are standing in the room when I enter. They stop arguing and stare at me.

The woman's brow furrows as she scans my visible flaws. She tries to approach me, and Carmine steps in the middle.

"Just a quick exam," she offers. "Five minutes. That's all I'm asking."

"Marco, please excuse us so Dr. Pierce may examine Mia," Carmine requests.

"Of course," Marco nods and leaves us.

The woman closes in on me, and I take a small step back. Her intentions are clear, but Carmine's stern face and posturing make me nervous.

"Mia, I'm Dr. Pierce. I'm here to check your injuries."

My eyes dart from one inanimate object to another, unsure of what to do. I move away further when Carmine positions himself beside the doctor.

"Mia, remove your clothes." Carmine orders.

"That won't be necessary," Dr. Pierce points out. "The exam can be done with them on."

Carmine ignores her and rips my sweatshirt off, pulling my hair with it. He grabs my underwear and whips them down to the floor. I cover my bloody private area. Dr. Pierce covers her mouth and shuts her eyes.

A single tear slips from my lid, and Carmine swipes it away. "There, Dr. Pierce, now you can see everything. You have five minutes," he says, clicking a timer on his phone and resting his hands behind his back.

Dr. Pierce works me over from top to bottom, taking my blood pressure, pulse and listening to my lungs.

She presses on the bruises around my ribs, making me wince. "When did this happen?"

"Last week," I cry.

"Carmine, she is in no shape to take the beatings you are giving her. If you're not careful, she'll end up in the hospital or worse."

"If it happens, it happens. Besides, isn't that what you're here for?" Carmine shrugs as though her warning doesn't matter.

Dr. Pierce places her hands in her blue dress pants. Her paisley silk shirt is wrinkle-free and has pleasant blue, yellow, and green colors. The timer beeps, making me jump.

Carmine presses a button, and the noise stops. "That will be all, Dr. Pierce."

Our eyes meet, and mine plead with her for help I know she can't provide. Not if she values her life. Carmine steps over to the door and opens it. The doctor takes the hint and walks slowly away.

Marco peers inside the room, and his jaw drops at my battered flesh. "Jesus, Carmine. What have you done?"

"Don't be ridiculous. Most of this is from the accident," he insists.

Carmine turns Marco away from me as they move into the hall. "Mia, get dressed," Carmine barks over his shoulder as he locks me in.

More intense fighting comes from the other side of the wall as I fumble into my top. There are many voices. Someone new has joined in the argument as I sit on the bed.

The door rattles, and an unfamiliar man, wearing multiple gold rings on his fingers, enters the room. They glimmer under the chandelier as he waltzes toward the bed and sinks into the leather chair beside me. His hair is salt and pepper, with a clean-shaven face, and his eyes are brown with long lashes.

He turns the seat so he's facing me. "Mia, my name is Dominic Pirelli. Welcome to my home."

This man is the boss. He is the equivalent of Carmine and is Marco's father. A head peeks in the entrance, grabs the knob, and shuts the door giving us privacy.

"I'm sorry for what you are going through. But you need to understand, rules are rules. Do I agree with Carmine's method of punishment for you? Well, no. I would have killed you and saved my energy. But my son likes you, and Carmine needs you, so here we are at an impasse.”

Tears return and flow like a river. No matter how hard I try to shut the waterworks off, they continue dripping from my face.

“Please make him stop. I’ll do anything you ask. I just can't take any more of this torture."

“It is not for me to decide when your punishment ends. Carmine has lost his son, and you are to blame.”

“Tony killed him. Not me.”

“That’s where you are wrong, Mia. When you left, it created a ripple, affecting everyone. If you didn’t leave Nicoli, none of this would have happened. He would have never left the sanctity of his home. So quit claiming you’re an innocent victim in all this. You broke the rules,” Dominic points out as he stands. “The best I can do is guarantee he won’t hurt you under my roof.”

“And if he doesn’t honor your wishes?”

Dominic didn’t reply. A smile spreads across his face as he belly laughs and exhales through parted lips. He continues chuckling as he taps on the door, and someone lets him out.

I gaze down at my hands. The knuckles of my fingers are white from gripping the sheets. The fabric stays wrinkled as I release it and shake the life back into my appendages. Carmine can’t hurt me here.

The plan needs to change. Baiting Carmine into hurting me may be the way to go instead of seducing Marco. If the punishment for breaking your word is what I think it is, Dominic will kill Carmine for disrespecting his home. Then I wouldn't be indebted to Marco for anything and may be able to leave.

I managed to smile, but it split my lips open again.

Blaire enters, sets a lunch tray down on the dresser, and passes me a napkin. “That’s going to happen every time you try and smile. You know that, right?”

“Yes.”

"What are you smiling about anyways?"

A puff of air shoots out of my nose. "New plan," I say, dabbing my bloody mouth with the white cloth. "Want to hear it?"

"Do tell," she whispers and leans closer.

Chapter Thirty-Two
Push

The plan is simple. Putting it in motion, however, may be detrimental to my health.

Blaire thinks seducing Marco would be less risky, but I don't want to owe anyone anything. Dominic told Carmine that keeping me confined was not in his best interest. I'm allowed to wander as I please since almost every room has a camera and security throughout the house.

Over the last several days, Carmine has worked with Marco and his men to find Tony and get the other house he owns in order. If it keeps him away from me, I'm happy.

The library is my favorite place to hang out. Marco has an extensive collection of books. Though it's his home, Dominic keeps ownership of it until the day he dies. I remove a thick hardcover from the shelf and sink myself into a plush black leather chair.

"One of my favorites." Marco points out as he enters.

"Same. I haven't read it in years."

He sits across from me and opens a book of his own. We stay silent, enjoying each other's company without saying a word. Every so often, I peek over, and Marco does the same. This is not part of the plan anymore. But it can't hurt to create a safety net in case my idea fails.

My fingers rub the inner part of my thigh as Marco stares. He smiles with his eyes as I flip pages and stroke my skin. I move my hand to my lips and tug my lower lip using my pointer. It hurts, but it's worth it to gain his attention.

"Do you read often?"

"In my free time," Marco says, resting his book on his lap. "You?"

"Not as much as I once did, but I hope things will change."

"What things?" Carmine asks as he stops beside me.

Shit...he's ruining my chance to build a rapport with Marco. Carmine's thumb and pointer fingers glide over each other in a circle as he waits for my response.

"Having more time to read," I answer without breaking eye contact with Marco.

"Stand up," Carmine orders.

To begin being defiant now would give me away too fast. I need to pace my actions to build up a slow and eventual response from Carmine. I do as he asks. He takes my book, places it on the coffee table, and pulls me back onto his lap.

Marco averts his eyes as Carmine slides his hands up my shorts and rubs the front of my underwear. I grab his wrists and pull them out. My thumbs are feeling better, but still weaken my grip.

Carmine squeezes my arms and throws them aside. He sticks them back inside my bottoms, this time being rougher.

"Enough," Marco shouts.

"Oh, Marco, I'm not hurting her."

"Mia, please excuse us."

Carmine allows me to stand, but I hesitate. Marco senses my reluctance and guides me to the open doorway.

As soon as the door shuts, shouting echoes through the halls. Blaire passes me as I eavesdrop. "What's happening?"

"They're arguing."

"Well, you work fast," she smiles. "Come on, let's go pick your outfit for dinner."

An assortment of dresses dangles from a rack provided by a delivery service. Blaire and I sort through the options one at a time. A silver, off-the-shoulder A-line glimmers in the light as it rocks on its hanger. I remove it and gaze at its quality fabric.

"Try it on," Blaire says.

I remove my T-shirt and shorts and hike the dress up from the floor.

Blaire zips up the back and turns me around. The attire floats over my curves like lava down a mountain. The lines of my panties poke through, making it less sexy. Wearing a thong is possible, but those lines would also show. The material is beautiful but thin.

"Commando may be your best bet," Blaire giggles.

"No way," I laugh. "Help me take this off so I can get cleaned up."

Blaire tosses the shimmering attire over her arm and stares at my battered body.

"What?"

"He's done so much to you," she sighs, caressing the bruise by my partially closed eye. "I'm sorry."

"It's not your fault," I smirk, splitting my lip again. "The bruises will fade with time."

Blaire yanks a tissue from a dispenser on a side table and dabs my lip. "This is why he struck you in the mouth. This is going to bleed every damn time you smile."

"He doesn't want me to be happy."

"Carmine wants everyone to share in his misery. If he can't be happy, no one can."

Someone from the kitchen interrupts our moment, and Blaire steps away. I pull on my shorts and t-shirt and head to the guest bedroom to clean up.

The hot shower stings my bruised body as it beats down on me. The water turns scorching as someone flushes the toilet. I scream and turn the knob off. When I move the curtain aside, Carmine sits on the closed seat.

Keeping myself covered, I reach for the towel on the bar. "Did you use the toilet, or were you just being cruel?"

Carmine didn't reply. He gazes around the room from one corner to the next, and a sinister smile creeps across his face. *Cameras.*

The bathrooms have none. His fingers pinch the white partition. The hooks holding up the material screech to the side as Carmine climbs in, still clothed. He backs me against the wall and draws the fabric back into place.

"Please, don't," I beg as he comes closer.

Carmine places his palms on my bare waist. His thumbs massage my iliac crest as he rests his head on my left breast.

"Your heart is pounding. Are you afraid?"

"Yes," I whisper.

"In a few days, we are leaving for the vacation home. When we arrive, I'm planting my seed right here," he says, cupping my vagina with his fingers. "Say yes," he insists, holding my crotch hostage.

"No!" I say, pushing him away.

Carmine grabs my pubis bone from the inside of my body and throws my backside into the wall. "Say yes to later, and I can go easy on you. If I take you now, it will be a painful experience."

I remain silent until he whips his fingers out of me and yanks out his rock-solid erection. My eyes widen, and I push it away.

"Yes," I cry out. "Later is fine."

A satisfied smile spreads over his face. It is the moment he has been waiting for. His hand caresses my breast as he leans in for a kiss which I refuse to accept. I thought he might punish me for this, but he doesn't. He has what he needs from me. Permission. Hurting me is no longer necessary.

The curtain clanks to the left as he steps out and gazes at his reflection in the mirror. His manhood prevents him from leaning against the vanity. A piece of lint hangs from his mustache, and he plucks it out before whistling away with his appendage still dangling outside his dress pants.

I sink to the bottom of the tub and scream on my hands and knees. There is little time now. A few days is all I have left to change the course of my future. I need to work fast.

Marco and I have books in common, and I can use our love for them to entice and seduce him. Dominic is hosting a dinner party on the patio for some of his long-standing business partners and family tonight. It is the only chance I may have to put my plan in motion. I stare down at my shaking hands and clench my fists. Bravery has never been my strong suit, but facing a lifetime of misery is a powerful motivator.

Chapter Thirty-Three
What Happens in the Car

The silver outfit sparkles under the lights of my reflection. Blaire curls my hair and cascades it over my left shoulder. Earlier in the evening, she placed a cold compress on my eye to reduce the swelling further. Once she applied makeup, the evidence of Carmine's abuse is barely noticeable.

Dinner is in an hour, but I'm eager for the night to begin. I scoop up my heels from the area rug and saunter barefoot down the hall.

Marco catches a glimpse of me as I pass the library. "Mia?"

"Yes?"

"Wow. That's some dress," he says.

Marco jogs to catch up to me when I continue walking. I take a wine goblet from the cupboard, and Marco holds the bottle. His eyes don't leave mine as the cup overfills onto the tile. "Shit," he says, wiping the floor with a towel.

My fingertips brush against his forehead as he opens his mouth to speak but can't find the right words.

Carmine's voice pierces the silence between us. "What are you doing? No alcohol."

Marco stands as Carmine snatches the glass and rests it on the counter. "Mia, come with me."

I roll my eyes as I fall in line behind Carmine and shoot Marco a playful wink. Inside, I'm proud of myself. Never in my life have I pursued anyone. Everyone chased me. Being naughty is exciting.

The color drains away from my skin as Carmine leads me outside. A car is waiting with the door ajar, and I stagger back.

"Are we leaving?"

"Not the property, only the house," he says.

Fuck

Dominic said Carmine couldn't hurt me under his roof.

Carmine seizes me around the waist and forces me into the vehicle. I grab the handle on the opposite side, and Carmine yanks me away. The driver raises the tinted partition between us and rolls away from the house.

"Do you take me for a fool, Mia? Just because I'm preoccupied doesn't mean I don't hear things. Did you think you could turn Dominic and Marco against me by forcing me to lay hands on you? Playing games with me is not something you want to do."

"I don't know what you're talking about."

"Liar," Carmine screams, grabbing me by the hair.

I swing and land a punch on the side of his face. His eyes open to saucers, and I cover my head, but his fist punches my inner thighs, one then the other, making them useless, painful noodles.

I bawl as he takes my head in his palms and hollers in my face. "If you ever hit me again, I'll fucking kill you. Do you understand?"

"Yes."

Car headlights shine through the tinted windows, and Carmine sits back. The guests are arriving for dinner, so he doesn't have time to finish what he started.

Carmine sighs beside me. The driver circles the house and stops.

The door opens, and Dominic peers inside. "Carmine, might I have a word?"

Carmine nods to Dominic but doesn't exit right away. He turns to me and places his arm on the back seat's headrest.

"Mia, tonight you are to remain quiet. Don't speak to anyone, not even Blaire. As for Marco, keep your hands to yourself. I don't want to kill you, but it may be my only option if you keep pushing your luck."

Carmine exits and joins Dominic. I would have run if my legs worked. Instead, I scoot out of the car and stand.

My muscles fail, and I land hard on the concrete. Blood oozes from both my knees as I try again with the same result.

A woman in a red dress with brown hair pulled into a neat bun runs to my side. "Let me help you," she offers, wrapping her arm around my waist.

Right by the door is a waiting chair, and she drops me into it. "Is there anything I can do for you?"

Her husband joins her when I decline further help, and they head to the back of the house where the party is.

Marco appears on the staircase and hustles down them. "Mia, what happened?"

My upper half sways in the seat as I remain soundless. If I answer, I die. Marco rests his hand on my knee, and I shove it off. His eyes grow dark as he peers around the room. Without warning, he scoops me up, carries me into the library, and lowers me onto the leather couch.

"Mia, tell me what he did," he insists, locking the door and pulling up a chair. "Did he hurt you?"

I'm unsure why I dared show him what Carmine did to me. I lift my dress, revealing the massive inner thigh bruises that are forming.

Marco shakes his head and clears the desktop of its writing supplies. "Bastard. My father gave him an order."

"Not in the house," I murmur.

"What?"

"He did it in the car, not the house," I cry.

"Fucking loopholes," he huffs.

The doorknob jiggles. I exchange glances with Marco, and my body starts shaking.

Dominic steps inside when Marco unlocks the door. "Son, why are you behind locked doors with Carmine's future wife?"

"I have concerns for her safety," Marco explains.

"I understand, but unless he breaks my rules, there is nothing we can do. Come, dinner is served."

"But he has." Marco points out.

"According to who? Her? Did you see it? Is it on camera?"

"No. But she has injuries that..."

"Enough, Marco. I'm starving, and the food is getting cold."

Marco gazes at me one last time and leaves me alone with Dominic.

He sits across from me and crosses his legs. His thumb taps the top of his kneecap. I don't know where Marco gets his looks. His father is short and round with acne scars pitting his face.

"Did you hear me say dinner is ready?" Dominic asks, leaning forward.

I nod but won't make eye contact. Staying mute makes me appear disrespectful. Dominic stands and glares down at me.

"I asked you a question, and I expect a verbal response," he orders.

A pen and notepad are on the floor, and I pick them up and jot down an explanation. Dominic glances at the note, shreds it, and stalks out of the room.

I'm unsure how much time passed, but no one came for me. I need to pee, so I force myself to a standing position. My legs wobble as I stumble out of the room. Using the wall for leverage, I slide against the chevron wallpaper and slip into a half bath.

It's quiet, cozy, and warm here. No one else can fit in this tiny room. My body leans on the sink base, and I fall asleep on the toilet.

Chapter Thirty-Four
The Silent Treatment

The door creaks open, and an unfamiliar woman jiggles my shoulder. They've been searching for me. Not just Carmine and Marco, the whole damn dinner party is standing outside the bathroom.

Blaire wedges in the doorway and rests her palm on my brush-burned knee. "Mia, are you okay?"

I gaze at the many faces behind her, but my eyes are set on only one, Carmine. His head shakes, and his eyes are angry. My fingernails click as I fidget with them in my lap. *'Am I okay?'* What kind of question is that?

Multiple people whisper to each other as Carmine moves them aside and comes closer.

My orders are to remain silent, so I keep my lips sealed. A hand squeezes Blaire's shoulder, and she backs out of the entrance.

Carmine kneels before me, and I lean away. "Mia, get up."

I grasp the hand towel ring, and it rips out of the wall when I try to use it to stand. Pieces of drywall float down onto my dress. I gawk at the anchor and screw that once filled the hole.

"Stupid girl," Carmine screams, yanking me out of the bathroom.

"Stop," Dominic orders. "It's not her fault. It has been loose for some time."

Carmine let me go, and I rested my butt against the door frame. He places his hands on his hips and glares at me.

Dr. Pierce presses through everyone and stoops down. She sets a bowl of soapy water and a bag on the floor. Dominic disperses the crowd behind her and directs them back to the dining area. Only Dr. Pierce, I, and Carmine remain.

"Mia, I'm going to clean these and put some ointment on them," she says as she dabs them. "Carmine noticed your empty seat at the table. We were worried. Are you dizzy?"

I shake my head but don't talk. She peers over her shoulder at Carmine's twisted face and sighs. "Must you hover?"

"Mia's my future wife, and her health concerns me. So yes, I'm hovering."

The doctor stands after applying a bandage to each of my kneecaps.

Her face comes within a foot of Carmines. "If you're so concerned about her, might I suggest keeping your hands off her? Stressing her out and beating her causes anxiety, depression, and PTSD. Not only that, but the chances of you killing her are high. I know you blame her for Nicoli's death, but remember, she didn't pull the trigger. Like it or not, she loved him too. If you expect her to have your children and create an heir, I recommend using kindness. Forcing her into an arranged marriage with the father of her now deceased fiancé is a lot for anyone to absorb. Don't make it worse for you both by being cruel."

The doctor picks up her things and marches away. I keep my focus on the ground. Carmine didn't move at first. He takes his hand, swipes it over his face, and exhales.

With the tips of his fingers, he tilts my face level with his. "Our food is getting cold."

I roll my body away from him and toward the dining room. My pace is slow and annoys Carmine. It's his fault, and he knows it but would never admit it.

"Come here," he insists, scooping me up. "Not a fucking word at dinner. Understand?"

A knot rotates in my abdomen as I nod. Carmine carries me to the entrance, sets me down, and loops his arm around mine as he opens the double doors. He guides me to a chair on one side of a massive table for twenty guests.

A silver platter is set before me, and Carmine removes the lid. Underneath is my favorite meal, filet mignon with steaming mashed potatoes and Parmesan asparagus. This could be my last for all I know. I'd love to eat it, but current events have taken my appetite.

"Not hungry?" Marco asks.

The air in the room is suffocating me. It fills with watchful eyes and unspoken words as everyone waits for me to reply. I remain silent as ordered.

Everyone at the table is stuffing their faces and gulping down wine. How can they be so obtuse in their actions? Ignoring me. Ignoring what Carmine has done to me and continues to do. Where is their empathy and compassion? Have they been a part of this business and family for so long that they, too, are numb? They are no different than Carmine. I've never wished death on anyone. But as I stare at the emotionless faces of everyone sitting at this table, there is nothing more in the world that I want than to put a bullet between every one of their ignorant eyes. Even the woman who helped me at the entrance ignored me. I'm sure her husband played a part in that as he whispers for her to mind her business.

I feel Carmine beside me. Not physically, but the empathetic side of me takes in the emotions coming from him. Though I can't speak, my body does it for me. Without warning, my fist bounces off the platter, flipping it over. All my senses turn off. There is no noise, no one around, no more smells. My eyes are open, but I can't see. A sharp pain in my chest startles me, and I grip it. I have a private earthquake, and every guest at the table gawks at me like an episode of Nova. Their eyes dart from one face to the next. No one stands from their seats. Some continued eating while others eyed Carmine. My eyes search the room for Blaire, but I can't find her. I need help.

Carmine places his palm on my arm, but his touch makes everything worse. My teeth chatter as a voice to my right speaks, but I can't understand what she's saying.

"Mia, you're having a panic attack. I need you to take slow, deep breaths. I'm here to help," Dr. Pierce explains. "Let go of the knife, and we can leave the room."

Her words confuse me. What knife? I gaze at my right hand when she rests hers on it. A blade meant to cut steak is tapping the glass beside it as I tremor. I release it, and tears flood my cheeks as I continue to shake. The clanking of my teeth grew louder and louder. Soon it is all I can focus on.

Dr. Pierce turns to Carmine, "I warned you."

"Get up, Mia," Carmine hisses as he drags me out of my seat.

The blood-curdling scream from the depths of my broken mind causes everyone to cover their ears. His face pales as I grab a salad bowl and launch it across the room, missing Dominic's head. Something stabs me in the leg, and my eyes cross as Dr. Pierce removes a needle. My body floats to the floor like a molted feather from a flying bird.

The ceiling tiles spin above me as I lay helpless on the rug. Dr. Pierce and Carmine hover over my paralyzed frame. His face twists with disgust as my eyes flutter. He hates me, and I don't blame him. I hate myself, too, but for a different reason. All the red flags were there when I met Nick, but I chose to ignore them. If I had just walked away when he gave me the chance, I'd be at work right now and have control of my future.

"I'm sorry," Dr. Pierce whispers as I fade into the darkness.

Chapter Thirty-Five
Repercussions

Awakening in a pitch-black room disorients me. The covers slip away from my hip, and a cool breeze chills my naked skin.

An arm drapes across my waist. Carmine's nude body spoons mine. The breathing over my shoulder is soft and shallow. He's sleeping.

I reach down to check for underwear, but I'm not wearing any. The weight of his hand is uncomfortable, so I push it off me.

"Nothing happened. You've been asleep for over ten hours. I started to wonder if Dr. Pierce put you in a coma."

"I wish she did."

Carmine turns me onto my back and climbs on top of me. He interlaces his fingers with mine and hovers over me.

"Soon, we are leaving for the house. I didn't intend on hurting you when you relinquish yourself to me, but after last night's meltdown, I changed my mind."

"Why not do it now?" I ask, pushing against his palms.

"In my home, I do what I like. When you scream, no one will care or try to save you."

Carmine rotates his massive erection against my pelvis as he moans. I slide myself toward the headboard, but he pulls me back by the shoulders and continues grinding—a tiny sliver of light peeks through the curtain and blinds me. The sun is coming up, and a new day is beginning. This is it. This is my last chance to save myself from a lifetime of misery with Carmine. My pelvis hurts from his persistent humping.

"I have to use the bathroom," I say, disrupting his momentum.

"I'm not finished with you," he glares.

"If you don't move, I'll piss on you."

"You wouldn't dare."

"Try me," I murmur.

Carmine huffs and moves aside. I move the drape open further so I can see. A dark gray, button-up shirt rests over a corner chair. I stuff my arms into it to cover myself. Carmine keeps his eyes on me as I cross in front of the footboard.

"Come here."

"No, I told you, I need to pee."

He rolls out of bed, grabs my arm, and tugs at the shirt I just put on. "This is mine."

The shirt falls to the floor as he pushes it over and off my shoulders. I sense his eyes on my backside as I turn to walk away from him. He seizes my hips from behind and pulls me back to him. It wasn't about the shirt. His mouth presses against the small of my back. He licks me from that point to my neck as he stands and moves my hair aside. His fingers comb through my pubic hair.

"This will need to go."

I push him away from me with my buttocks, and he doesn't object. Now he wants to shave me. For what? His convenience. I think not. I hope you choke on it.

"Asshole," I whisper under my breath as I open the bathroom door.

"What did you say?"

"Nothing," I lie as I close the door.

Next to the toilet is a pale pink towel and washcloth. On the counter is a blue sundress, bra, and lace panties to match. Carmine chose the outfit, no doubt.

I turn the shower on hot and climb in. I expected Carmine to make an appearance, but he never joined me. The clothes he picked fit, but I didn't care for the length of the dress. When I bend over, my underwear shows, leaving nothing for the imagination. At first, I thought about telling Carmine, but I realized this may be to my benefit.

I brush my teeth, floss, use mouthwash, and apply a little makeup. Carmine is gone when I reenter the bedroom. In my head, I imagine him wandering the halls nude. Since this isn't his home, I hope he puts on a robe. When I try to leave, the door won't open. Carmine locked me in.

"What the… argh."

Fresh air floats in from the open balcony door. The room is only two stories from the concrete, so I may survive if I fall. It's worth it to me as I toss my sandals over and climb the railing onto the next landing.

A bed sits empty to my right, but someone just turned off the shower. I tiptoe to their door.

"Mia, how did you get in here?" Marco says as he appears wet and wearing only a towel.

"Carmine locked me in, so I scaled the balcony."

Now is my chance to make a pass. I drop a sandal and bend over to pick it up. My hand misses it several times, and I bounce my cheeks with every attempt.

When I turn around, Marco is in my airspace. His hands reach under my dress, grip my behind, and pull against his erection.

"Mia, you are a tease," he whispers as he shoves his tongue down my throat, tears my panties aside, and rams his fingers inside me.

"You're hurting me," I say as he forces them in further.

He lifts me off the floor and slams me onto the mattress. The rest of my underwear is torn away, cutting my skin as he rips them off.

"Marco, stop."

"I want you, Mia."

"Carmine threatened to hurt me if I even speak to you."

"I can handle Carmine."

Marco strokes my cheek and grinds his toweled loins into me. "Just the tip, Mia. I need you." He moans as he removes his towel.

"No," I huff and push him off me.

Marco rolls his eyes, smacks his lips, and glares at his erection. I peek at it as well. His short, fat penis reminds me of an undersized honey nut squash. For some reason, the thought of him touching me with it makes me nauseous.

"Fuck," he groans, climbing off me. "You're going to leave me like this?"

"I have no choice."

More like I don't want him or his manhood anywhere near me. My gut tells me Marco is a violent lover who, once Carmine is out of the way, won't take no for an answer. I use one finger to lift my underwear off the floor and press my ear to the door. The hall is quiet, so I tiptoe out of Marco's room unnoticed. The balled-up panties are still in my hand, so I stuff them in a trash can in the kitchen.

Carmine strolls in wearing black silk pajama pants. His eyes turn dark and angry.

"Who let you out?"

"I let myself out, Carmine. I'm not an animal."

"Go back to your room," he orders.

"I'm hungry and need caffeine. Want some?" I offer, holding up the pot.

He crosses the room and takes the carafe from my grasp. A mug I intended to use drops to the floor and breaks in half. I bend at the waist before him, exposing my bare buttocks as Marco enters.

"Mia, stand up," Carmine yells. "Where are your underpants?"

"I threw them out," I smirk. "They didn't cover much, so I decided not to wear them.

Blaire strolls in and stops. She glances from Carmine to me to Marco and back again. "What's happening?"

"Mia needs new underwear. Please take her to our room and help her find some," Carmine says without breaking eye.

Blaire nods and says nothing as we stroll away.

She peers over her shoulder and whispers, "Mia, what is happening?"

"Marco tried to have his way with me in his room."

"What? How did you end up in there?"

"Doesn't matter."

"Is he taking care of Carmine?"

"I hope so," I say, raising my eyebrows.

Blaire smiles as she locks the bedroom door. "Carmine is in a mood today. I tried to ask him questions about our plans for today, and he snapped at me. Be careful."

"I will."

"Good. This will be all for nothing if you get yourself killed."

Chapter Thirty-Six
Trigger

After finding new panties, I sit on the patio with a novel. The sun warms my aching muscles and lifts my mood.

Despite being in pain from various injuries, and Marco's forcible touching, I'm having a fabulous day. He should be discussing his plans with Dominic by now. This time tomorrow, Carmine should be dead. I turn the page of my book and sigh. The heroine in this story is so much stronger than I am. She's intelligent, funny, and brave. Sometimes I wish I had never left Nick. None of this would be happening.

I stared at the gazebo Nick wanted to marry me under. Dominic's property is much more scenic than Carmines. In my mind, Nick kisses me to seal our fate, scoops me up, and carries me across the threshold. As I play the scene in my head, Nick's face dissolves and turns to Tony's. I twitch between my legs as the memory of our time together comes rushing back. Tony is out there somewhere, planning his next attack.

A mower powers up nearby, distracting me from my reading. The landscaper plows over the lush lawn, shooting blades of green onto the concrete.

A dust cloud of dry pollen and cut grass floats into my nostrils. The tingle in my sinuses hits me, and a barrage of sneezes follows. One, another, and another. They keep coming. I'm up to ten in a row before they stop, and my eyes swell. My sight is limited to tiny slits as I fumble over furniture. The last time I suffered this type of response was in high school.

I wave my arms in front of me, searching for the house or something to guide me.

Someone's hands engulf my head, but I don't recognize the blurry face.

"Mia, what happened," Marco asks as he wipes my eyes.

"Allergic reaction."

He picks me up, brings me inside, and hustles past Carmine on his way to Dr. Pierce's room.

"What did you do to her," Carmine hollers, yanking me from Marco's grasp.

"Nothing," Marco says as they each hold one of my arms.

Dr. Pierce runs into the hallway when she overhears the arguing. Marco pulls me away from Carmine, passes Dr. Pierce, and sits me in the chair.

"No. Lie her down over there," Dr. Pierce points.

Carmine pushes Marco when he comes to move me, and Marco shoves him back.

"Don't fucking touch my wife," Carmine screams, shoving him again.

"You're not married yet," Marco hisses in Carmine's face.

Dr. Pierce chimes in. "If you two are planning on continuing this fight, I suggest you get the hell out of my room."

Marco chooses the higher road and leaves. I sense Carmine standing next to me. Though my sense of sight is almost non-existent, my other senses take over. His nose breathing and intermittent huffing send my stomach into a frenzy. He's angry.

Carmine takes me from the seat and lays me on the bed. The moment his skin touched mine, I felt a strong urge to vomit. He wants to hurt me but can't. The doctor places a cold compress across my eyes as another round of sneezing begins. Snot shoots out of my sinuses like a depressurized volcano. Slimy goop is on the crook of my forearm as I try and control the radial spray. Twelve sneezes later, and my face resembles a kindergartener with a virus.

"Why won't they stop?" Carmine asks.

"Whatever set them off is still in her sinuses. Mia, I'm putting an antihistamine mist in your nose. It should help some, but I also want you to swallow these pills."

I open my mouth, and Dr. Pierce sets in two capsules. She sticks a wad of tissues in my hand so I can blow out the allergens. The more I blew, the more came out. After going through half a box of tissues, the sneezing ended.

"Mia, you need to stay in the house until the air clears. Otherwise, it may happen again."

Carmine leans onto the mattress after the doctor leaves and squeezes my cheekbones. "What did I say about talking to Marco?"

"Carmine, I needed help. It shouldn't matter where it came from."

"Mia, I forgive you this time, but in the future, I want you to listen and do as you're told."

The mattress shifts and his footsteps disappear, but he leaves the door open. I'm alone, lying on the doctor's comforter, blind and vulnerable. I reach down and adjust my clothes. Until my sight returns, I'm at everyone else's mercy. Carmine's forgiveness isn't without consequence; it never is.

As I lie motionless, I picture myself lying next to the ocean with a cold washcloth across my face. The waves crash over my feet, exfoliating them. I take off my blindfold, and in the distance, multiple people fish from the wooden pier. Sand fills in between my toes as I walk along the shore carrying my sandals. I may stand before a vast sea someday, but it's a fantasy now.

When my face is numb, I remove the ice pack, and reality returns. The swelling is better, but my eyes still itch and burn. Next to me is a container of eye drops. I drip some in each eye and sit up.

My sinuses are full, so I clear them again before leaving. I shuffle my way to the library, where Marco talks to his father. There is an awkward pause when I enter.

"Sorry, I can come back."

"Don't be silly, Mia. Take a seat," Dominic says, offering me his chair. "Are you okay?"

"I guess so."

Dominic nods his head and raises his eyebrows. "Well, I have some things to do. You two should talk."

The door swings shut behind him as Marco stands. I cower beneath his stature as he leans over and kisses the top of my head. My swollen eyes meet his as he hovers above me. After a long awkward pause between us, he strolls over and locks the door.

Chapter Thirty-Seven
Crossing the Line

Marco takes my hand and helps me to my feet. I stare at a piece of shredded paper on the carpet, avoiding eye contact with him.

"Mia, look at me," he says as he slides his hands around my waist.

"I can't."

I break from his grasp and fumble with the locked door. He reached for me as I swung it open and hustled into the hallway. Seducing or allowing any physical touching will be in vain if Carmine doesn't see it happen.

Blaire rounds a corner and snags me. "Mia, I'm glad I found you. Carmine is packing the car. We are leaving."

"What? When?"

"Right now."

"Shit. Where is he now?"

"He's saying goodbye to Dominic, and after, he's coming for you."

"Find him, and when he asks where I am, tell him," I say as I head back to the library.

Marco was still sitting in his leather chair when I burst into the room. It's now or never, I convince myself as I toss the book he's reading in the air and climb on his legs. I shove my tongue down his throat as he lifts my dress and grips my backside. Marco hardens under me as I rock on his lap. The door slams open behind me.

"Fucking whore," Carmine screams as he yanks me off Marco's lap and into the hallway.

My arms and legs flail every which way as I scream. Carmine drags me out of the house and throws me onto the lawn.

"You want a cock so bad; now you're getting one," Carmine hisses as he unbuttons his pants.

I find my footing and take off running toward the tree line. Something strikes me in the back of the head, and I fall. Carmine hobbles to a stop, wearing only one shoe. I crawl away from him, but he seizes me. My neck cracks as he whips it back and tears off my underwear.

"Nooooooo," I scream and throw my head into his face.

Carmine lets go, and I scramble to my feet. Blood drains out of his nose as he lunges for me. My feet make quick backward steps, but I can't get away in time. He strikes me hard on the side of the head. Black spots bounce before my eyes as Carmine climbs on me and spreads my legs. My disorientation subsides enough for me to see a group of men, including Marco and Dominic, coming up behind him. Carmine doesn't realize what's about to happen, but I do.

I shut my eyes as Carmine's manhood touches the outside of me, ready to enter. It is the closest he will ever come to taking me. The loud discharge of a gun forces my eyes open.

A bullet strikes Carmine in the back, and he rolls away from me. My heels dig into the dirt as I scurry away from the hail of bullets riddling his body.

It's over.

My eyes fix on his motionless corpse as more gunfire follows. Dominic and Marco's soldiers kill the rest of Carmine's men. I glance over my shoulder. The woods are at my back. If I turn around and run, I may have a chance.

Dominic is kneeling before me when I return my attention to the lawn of death. He offers me his hand, "You're a part of this family now. Carmine can't hurt you anymore."

After pulling me to a standing position, Dominic brushes the loose grass from my arms. "Marco, come help your future wife."

Future wife.

I knew this would happen. The only thing I have done is trade Satan for Lucifer. Exchanging one life for another. One problem at a time, I say to myself.

Dominic pulls out his phone and brings it to his ear. "Carmine is dead. Come see me tonight."

I step back and wonder who he's talking to as Marco steadies me with his frame. Blaire hurries to my side, tucks her head under my arm, and leads me away from him.

"What are you doing?" Marco asks as he rushes ahead of us.

"Mia needs a bath and fresh clothes," Blaire insists as she tries to usher me around him.

"I can handle it," he says, smiling as he hoists me off the ground and carries me to the entrance.

"Please, Marco. Blaire can help me. After I am ready, we can have a family dinner, and you can have me for dessert," I offer, stroking his hair. "Please."

He stops walking, sets me down, and sticks his tongue so far down my throat, I almost gag. "I can't wait. Blaire, take Mia to my room and help her."

"Of course," she smiles, taking me by the elbow.

Blaire glances over her shoulder as we enter the house. "Jesus, Mia. That was close."

"I know. What do we do now?"

"Don't worry. It is all taken care of."

"Why can't you tell me everything?"

"If I tell you, it may not work. Everyone needs to believe you."

"Believe me about what?"

"Mia, you ask too many questions," Blaire huffs growing frustrated. "Get your ass ready. We are running out of time."

"Fine. You don't have to be so grumpy about it."

Blaire stares at me with a twisted face as I paw through an array of attire. She picks an ivory pant jumpsuit with gold zip up the front from the hanger and hands it to me.

"Pants? I thought a dress would be more appealing to Marco. He might become suspicious if I'm wearing something so formal."

"Not when he gets a sneak peek of what's underneath," Blaire winks as she pulls a sexy, pearl-accented bra and matching underwear out of the drawer. "It's a push-up."

After taking a long hot shower, Blaire helps me apply makeup and pins my hair into a fancy bun. I stretch the bra behind my back and, after a brief struggle, find all three hooks. Blaire removes a pair of diamond and pearl stud earrings from her pocket, puts them in my ears, and wraps a gold necklace around my throat. It dangles between my breasts and draws your eyes downward.

I gaze at my reflection as she sets spike heels by my feet, and I slip them on.

"Oh, goody. The wedding planner is here," I say to Blaire in the mirror.

"Don't be silly," she says, shaking her head. "You are the First Lady, for sure."

We burst into laughter as someone taps on the door with their fingers. Our eyes lock as Blaire strokes my upper arms. "Ready?"

"Let's do this," I smile and take her hand.

Chapter Thirty-Eight
Broken

Blaire and I part ways in the kitchen. I stand in the doorway, watching the staff.

The chefs are busy with the finishing touches for this evening's meal. The workers move almost in sequence from one side of the room to the other. They have their rhythm and way of doing things, and it works for them. Blaire sets a bottle in the ice bucket and carries it away.

A hand caresses my backside. Marco whispers into my ear, "This is an unexpected outfit. I thought you might choose something sexy and red."

I turn and push him into the room across the hall. Marco's eyes fixate on my chest as I take down my zipper. A sharp pain in my thumb slows me down but doesn't stop me. The slow reveal lights up his face as my lace-covered breasts pop out. He cups his hands over them and rotates them like a dial on the radio.

"What is below the waist is so much better."

"Let me see," Marco insists as he takes ahold of the zipper and pulls it toward the floor.

My fingers slide the jumpsuit aside so he can view his dessert.

Marco spins me and touches the front of my panties. "Why can't I have you as an appetizer?"

"Naughty boy. You'll ruin my plans for you," I smile as I zip up my outfit.

Marco hangs his head as I turn and leave him and his hard-on standing in the empty room. Most of the family is in the sitting room, waiting for the table to be set. Dominic calls me to his side and pats the chair to his left. I sit silently beside him as he chooses his words.

"Mia, my son has never expressed an interest in settling down and getting married until you came along. He's been engaged twice now and both times he's lost interest and never cared to be involved in the planning. But with you, he's already chosen the location of your honeymoon and picked out the colors for your wedding. Although the loss of Carmine is a tragedy, it puts my family in a strategic position. When his home burned to the ground, he brought all his cash assets here, including yours," Dominic smiles. "After you marry Marco and are with child, I plan to relinquish your portion to you."

"And Carmine's?"

"Our families shared everything at the beginning of our mutual partnership—money, women, business, enemies, etc. But when Carmine lost his wife, he became unstable. Carmine questioned what we did and how we did it. Many of us grew uneasy with his paranoia and emotional state. So, we took the necessary steps to protect ourselves, our family, and our business."

The doorbell rings and echoes through the halls. Dominic stands and shoves his hands in his pockets. "Walk with me."

I join him as he strolls in the direction of the front door. My heels clank on the marble as I round the corner and stop. Standing in the foyer is Tony, dressed in full tactical gear. A Glock sits in a holster at his hip, and a sniper rifle hangs from his neck.

"Tony? What the hell is going on?"

Dominic takes a bag from another guest and passes it to Tony. "One million dollars as agreed upon. It won't bring your brother back, but with Carmine and the rest of his men gone, our family can return to the old ways."

"Thank you, sir," Tony says, shaking his hand and gazing at me. "I'm sorry."

Tony turns and walks away, leaving me trapped in my new life. Marco puts his hand around my waist and kisses my neck. "He's a loose-end father. We should take him out while he's here."

Dominic places his hands behind his back and strolls over to me. "Mia, the man who walked out the door, used you. His mission or job rather was to bait Nicoli out of hiding and kill him. But when you didn't call him, Tony left an anonymous message informing one of Carmine's men of your whereabouts. Of course, he informed Nicoli, who then came for you and well you know the rest. Now I have full control of the business, Marco gets you, and Tony walks away, as agreed, a million dollars richer. Everyone wins."

"You're a liar. Tony wouldn't. He said he'd come for me."

"I'm sure he said and did many things to you. But in the end, the result is the same." Dominic nods to Marco.

Something weighted and metallic slides into my grasp. "No loose ends, Mia. Take your revenge," Marco whispers.

My hand tightens around the Taurus 9mm in my palm as Marco continues to taunt me. "He's heading for the trees. Do you see him?"

"Yes," I murmur as my hand tremors.

"You're not letting him get away with hurting you, are you?"

"I…"

"Mia, no one leaves, remember?"

Marco turns me around, cups my face in his grasp, and kisses me. "Kill him."

Chapter Thirty-Nine
Betrayal

I turned my attention to Dominic and the others in the room. Everyone has their eyes on me, including Blaire. This is happening, like it or not. I sense their expectations. The room falls quiet as Marco walks away from me to join the others.

The gun shakes in my hand. The more I thought about what Tony did, the more pissed off I became. Carmine told me Tony used me, but I didn't believe him. I thought he was just trying to hurt me. As my blood pressure rose, so did my courage. I whip the front door open and storm off into the darkness. The heels of my shoes sink into the damp evening grass. I kick them aside and sprint toward Tony.

As I close in on him, sticks and debris dig into my feet. He turns too late as I squeeze the trigger, striking him in the back right shoulder. His body spins around as he hits the ground and points his handgun at me.

"You fucking bastard," I scream, pointing the gun at his chest. "How dare you? I trusted you despite everything you did to me. Was it all a lie? Did you even care about me? Or was it all for show?"

"Mia, stop. It's all part of the plan," he says, fighting the pain to get to his feet.

"Plan? You used me to get to Nick, and you have the nerve to leave me here."

Tears burst from my eyes as heartache and betrayal flood through me, drowning me.

"Mia, listen…."

"No. I'm done listening," I yell, squeezing the trigger.

Tony plummets into the brush, and a lump develops in my throat. A rush of regret overwhelms me. I'm stuck in the blank place in my mind and my legs refuse to move me in any direction. The air around me applies pressure across every surface of my skin. Like a tabletop vice, it crushes me into a pulp. An anxiety attack is imminent. I can't stay here, but I can't go back either.

One would assume Tony's plan didn't include being dead. But then again, maybe he didn't expect me to have the stones to pull the trigger. If I'm being honest with myself, I didn't think I could do it either. My left eye is twitching, and my stomach joins it.

"Mia, is he dead?" Marco yells from the elevated decking.

What have I done? Tony gained vengeance for his brother and made money by killing Nick at my expense, so why should it matter to me? It shouldn't, but it does.

The gun and money drop to the earth as I collapse and scream. The truth is, it matters because even though he betrayed me, I fantasized about him rescuing me. But from where I'm standing, it appears as though it was all an act to carry out his plan.

I understand why he did it. If someone killed a family member of mine, I wouldn't hesitate. Unfortunately for me, I appear to only be an extra. I played my role, and now it's over. At least for Tony, it is. How lucky is he?

I turn my attention to the heavens and pray for death. Staying here and forcing me to marry Marco is the last thing I wanted to happen. This isn't supposed to be my life. This was not part of the plan. I should be on my way home right now.

The sky is coudy, making it difficult to see the stars. It didn't stop me from trying to find the North Star. Someday I hope it can help me find my way back home.

When I get up and turn around, the entire family and dinner party stand beside Marco on the deck. They stay silent, as I pick up Tony's payment and walk toward the house. Applause erupts as I step onto the driveway space. I glance up, and they all are smiling. In their eyes, Tony's death is a celebratory moment.

But not to me. I put my head down, ashamed of what I have become. A killer, no better than Nicoli, Tony, Carmine, or the rest of the bunch. I'm one of them now, and what does that say about me?

Marco meets me at the door and holds it open. Blaire's eyes meet mine with a solemn stare as I pass her the duffle.

"Well, now that the loose ends are tied up, let's eat," Dominic says as he directs us to the dining hall.

Marco slides a chair out beside him. His hand rests on my leg when my ass hits the seat cushion. Inside, I want to scream and stab him with my fork.

Blaire comes from the kitchen with the other staff and helps serve dinner. Every guest receives a glass of red wine, except for me. Nothing has changed. It's bad enough that Carmine and Nick refused to let me drink. Now Marco does the same. Condensation drips from my cup onto the tablecloth. It spreads out like a stone in a pond, growing as it absorbs.

Marco strokes my thigh. When I gaze at his lap, his manhood bulges through his bottoms. His fingers walk between my legs and press my crotch through my pants. He's desperate for my body. Groping me beneath the table isn't proper, so I remove his hand and place it on his leg.

A soft smile spreads across Blaire's face as she takes her chair across from me. Dominic doesn't like empty chairs. Since Carmine is dead and his seat is available, they offer it to her. She and I are the last link to the Castino family.

Dominic rises, holding his wine. "A toast to Mia and Blaire, our newest members. Welcome and salud."

Everyone raises their glasses and repeats, 'salud' as they suck their drinks.

"Tasty vino, Blaire. Where did you buy it?" Marco asks.

"It's an exotic blend."

"Fine. Keep your secrets," he says as he tops off his glass.

I'm not hungry and I don't know how anyone else can be either. This is all normal for them but not for me. Blaire nods to my plate, encouraging me to eat. I lift my fork and knife, and they rattle as I try and fail to cut a piece. Marco reaches over, takes them from me, and cuts my steak into several pieces.

Once again, someone is treating me like a child. He lifts a piece to my lips, and I take it from him.

The filet melts in my mouth—hints of butter and bits of spice dance across my tongue.

I cover my chin with my fingertips as I moan aloud. "This is the best steak I have ever eaten."

No one responded. Blaire keeps her attention on her plate as Dominic begins coughing at the far end of the table. He must have swallowed wrong I thought as I stuffed another bite into my mouth.

Moaning comes from other guests at the table. They, too, are enjoying their food. Marco's head falls into me, and I push him back. A few seconds later, choking came from him, and he fell into me a second time.

"Marco, what are you doing?"

He doesn't reply. Foam spills over his seizing lips as he tumbles around me and onto the carpet. Moaning and gasping noises become deafening as everyone at the table suffers an unknown illness. Everyone except Blaire and me.

"Oh my God," I cry out as I glance at Blaire.

She raises her eyebrow and takes another bite of beef. The metal of her fork scrapes across her teeth, giving me goosebumps.

One by one, they fall like dominoes. Some are grasping their chests, others holding their throats, struggling to breathe. Dishes crash in the kitchen as more bodies topple to the floor. My eyes dart around the room from one body to the next. They're dying, all of them. I move away from the table and rest my back against the wall. Blaire continues eating and drinking as though nothing is happening.

Marco stares up at me as he takes his last breath. His head drops to the side, and the room falls silent. Blaire sighs through her nose, brushes her red lips with a cotton napkin, and sips her water.

She rests her knife on her plate and frowns. "Sit down, Mia, and finish your food."

Chapter Forty
Death for Dinner

My chair staggers closer to the table as I pull it in and pick up my fork. Blaire slides her last piece of steak around in its juices and shoves it in her mouth.

I've lost my appetite. Everyone in the room is dead except for Blaire and me. This is the part she refused to tell me about.

Blaire pops the cork of a fresh bottle of wine and dumps my water on the body of the person lying on the floor beside her. She fills my glass and hers to the top.

"Cheers, Mia," she says, taking a massive swig and setting it down. "Don't worry, this one is safe."

I lift my drink and sniff it as Blaire cuts her baked potato down the center. My hand tremors as I take a small sip and set it down.

Blaire breaks the silence between us. "Well, things didn't go how we hoped, but you're free now, which was our goal."

"What if Marco made me have wine?"

"Marco and I spoke before dinner. I told him you needed to be sober to serve him dessert."

I rest my elbows on the table and put my face in my palms. "If I knew this was part of the plan, I would never have…"

Blair's cell phone vibrates in her pocket. She peeks at the screen and stuffs it back inside. "You would never have what? Killed Tony? Yeah, I didn't see that coming either. He fell hard for y…"

Blair's voice trails off.

"What did you say?" I ask, getting up from the table. "Blaire, did you know Tony?"

"Dammit, Mia. What do you think? Tony's brother worked for Carmine, so of course, we had met before. This plan wasn't yours and mine. It was ours."

"Ours? Meaning Tony?"

"Yes, Tony. Don't you get it? Let me simplify it for you. When Carmine ordered Nicoli to kill Tony's brother, Dominic and Marco disagreed with the decision. Collecting money from a corpse, after all, is impossible, but Carmine wouldn't listen. When Tony came home for his brother's funeral, Dominic hired Tony to wipe out the Castino family and burn the entire empire to the ground. Then Sophie had an aneurysm. Nicoli wouldn't leave her side and you complicated things even further."

"Me? How?"

"Tony developed feelings for you. The more he did to upset you, the guiltier he felt. Cupid stabbed him in the ass with an arrow. After you two had sex, he became more determined," Blaire pauses and wipes butter from her chin. "Tony cornered me in the grocery store after Nicoli's death, and we discussed ways to get you out forever. As you can see, the plan worked. Everyone is dead, and you are free."

"Blaire, I shot Tony…twice. I thought he betrayed me. All this time, you two were working together?"

"I'm afraid so," she says, glancing at her phone again. "Time to go."

"Go? Blaire, there are dead bodies everywhere. Where are we supposed to go?"

Blaire hustles out of the room and returns with two duffle bags. She disappears a second time and comes back with a briefcase. My eyes dart from them, back to her.

Blaire lays the case down and opens it. Inside are stacks of hundred-dollar bills. She closes it and unzips a bag filled with jewelry. A ton of it. Diamonds, emeralds, and gold. The third one is Tony's, and it has a million dollars.

"There's more," Blaire grins. "Outside. Carmine didn't trust Dominic's men, so he left your cash and his in the car. There is a safe under the carpet. The cases Dominic's people carried have magazines in them."

Blaire picks up the briefcase and leaves the room. The front door opens, and a car beeps. I'm on the floor when she returns, weeping like a child.

"Mia, crying isn't helping. Now stand up and grab a bag. I'm too old to be hauling all this weight."

"Blaire, I'm a murderer," I whimper.

"And I'm a mass murderer. Now get your ass off the ground so we can go," she insists, grabbing me by the firearm.

I seize the handles of Tony's duffle and stumble along behind her. Blaire didn't bat an eyelash at the dead man lying across the walkway. The body blocks the door like a draft stopper, except he's not keeping out the cold. A hunting knife sticks out of his neck with his hand still on the handle.

A force field keeps me from crossing the threshold.

Blaire hoists her package into the trunk and scurries before the man. "Mia, close your eyes and take my hand."

I do as she asks, and she guides me over the corpse, but that's where I stop. Blaire's eyes follow mine to my bare feet. Dark red sticky liquid fills in between my toes.

All the hair on my arms stands on end. The shaking came on fast. Blaire pulls me toward her, trying to release me from the puddle, but I can't go. She takes the bag from me, tosses it in with the rest, and disappears around the side of the house.

"Bbbbblair…," I stutter as my mouth waters.

Vomit shoots from my nose and mouth like liquid through a cannon. Everything I've eaten since the third grade came out in several wrenching rounds.

Blaire appears with a hose and stops before the chunky puke pile. "Well, better now than in the car," she says, squeezing the handle.

Water blasts the base of my feet, stinging them. I jump away from the pain as she washes the stains of death from my soles. Blaire continues rinsing until all the evidence vanishes into the landscaping.

Blaire opens the back door and points, "Now, can we go?"

I shuffle to the opening and peek inside. It's empty, but not for long, as Blaire shoves me into the backseat by my ass cheeks. "Move it, Mia," she yells as sirens scream.

I slide to the far side behind the front passenger seat and lean against the window. Blaire hops in the driver's seat and floors the gas in a way that reminds me of Mrs. Baxter. I miss her, crazy as it sounds. Her cat annoys me, but she's a funny woman and a kind neighbor.

The car whips passed the chalet one last time before heading to the road that takes us to the highway. More dead bodies lay on the lawn as we entered the trees. Their eyes are empty, and their faces are bloody.

I gawk at Blaire and wonder how she could be so calm when she poisoned so many people. She rifles through her purse, pulls out a white, hand-rolled cigarette, and lights up. The smoke fills the vehicle, and I start coughing. The glowing amber of a doobie burns by my face as she passes a skunk smelling joint to me.

Now it makes sense, the smell I caught a whiff of emanating from her clothes and her bloodshot eyes. The way Carmine would cast a judgmental glance at her when he smelled it too.

"Take a hit. Trust me, it helps," she giggles, chokes, and exhales all at once.

I pluck it from her fingers and my eyes cross at the lipstick on the end of it. I'm going to regret this; I know it. My mouth wraps around the white paper, and I take a long deep draw of it.

"Fuck it," I say while holding my breath.

Chapter Forty-One
Freedom Isn't Free

I've never been a smoker or tried marijuana before, so I didn't know how I'd react to it. Blaire giggles from the front as I continue to cough.

"Mia, I think you've had enough," Blaire says, reaching into the backseat. "Pass it here."

I take a third quick hit and hand it to her. Blaire's eyes keep checking the rearview mirror as we wind our way down the private road. My body folds in on itself like a spider smacked with a rolled-up newspaper. If this is what a 'high' is meant to do to you, it may not be for me. Perhaps I did something wrong.

"Mia, are you okay back there? You are being too quiet."

"I think I'm dying."

"You're not. I promise. But you did hit the joint hard, though. I must say, I'm impressed you're still awake," she says exhaling a cloud of smoke.

"Are we near a store?"

"Mia, we are still driving on the private road. It's only been a few minutes. Do you have to pee?"

"No, but I'm starving and thirsty."

Blaire shakes her head as I rest mine on the seat. The skin on my scalp is tingling, and my neck is seconds away from popping off my shoulders. My body rocks forward and back, and I'm unsure if I'm making this motion or the car. My fingernails fold in half as I grip the leather to verify its existence.

Blaire slams on the brakes without warning, throwing me to the floor.

"Holy shit, Blaire. Where did you learn to drive?" I ask, pulling myself between the seats.

The door opens beside me, and Tony climbs in, bleeding from his shoulder.

"What the....," I slur as I try and focus on his face. "I am dead. Blaire, you lied to me."

"Mia, are you high?" Tony asks, lifting my sagging right eyelid.

"She's higher than my blood pressure is now. I almost hit your ass, you know," Blaire hollers toward the back.

Tony lifts my heavy head and sets it on his lap. The rest of me is still on the floor behind the passenger seat.

A tear slides down my cheek and onto his dirt-covered pants. "I'm sorry I killed you, but at least we are dead together."

"Mia, we aren't dead. I'm wearing a vest," Tony says, removing his bloody shirt.

The Velcro rips open as he undresses himself. Tony presses his hand against the exit wound on his shoulder. "Jeepers, Mia, did you have to shoot me?"

"Blaire, are we there yet? I'm so thirsty and need to eat food," I yell into the front.

The car makes a sharp turn, and my head rolls off Tony's lap and onto the floor next to his feet.

He sticks his face between his legs and stares down at me. "Mia, why don't you get up and I will strap you in."

"I can't because I'm too heavy," I whisper.

Tony shakes his head and sits back. I lay there, focused on the carpet and a piece of red lint.

"Blaire?"

"Yes, Mia."

"There's a fuzzy, and it's bugging me."

"That's nice, Mia. Why don't you shut your eyes, and we will wake you up when we find a store, okay?"

I thought I answered her, but I think it was all in my head. My memory is unreliable, and I'm not sure where I am or how I got there. I rest my face on a pair of filthy combat boots and my eyes droop close.

"Blaire?"

"What, Mia?"

"Are we dead? Is this why Tony is here? Because we both died."

"We made it—all three of us. We are free," Blaire explains.

I rotate my face to Tony's, and there are two of him. He shifts himself into the middle, reaches down, and uses his uninjured arm to help me off the floor.

I tuck my arm behind his back and wrap the other one around his waist, resting my head on his bare abdomen. "I'm sorry I shot you."

"No, Mia. I'm the one who should be apologizing. Things spun out of control so fast. Carmine hurt you, and it's my fault for not getting to you in time. I let revenge guide me instead of my heart. I put my mission before love."

"Love?"

"Yes, Mia. I love you."

"I love Yoo-hoo too. Are we at the store? I'm starving," I slurred.

"Tony, I think you need to wait and spill your guts until she's come off her high," Blaire laughs.

Tony strokes my hair and rests his palm on my hip. Blood leaches out from under his hand, and he applies more pressure. A trail of crimson liquid races down his stomach and disappears between us.

I pray inside my head that this isn't a hallucination from laced drugs. After everything we've been through to get here, everything we lost, wouldn't it be a cruel twist for this to be a lie or wishful thinking? A Ten of Swords tarot card was drawn at the end of the day. A premonition of disaster in our future. Except there are no cards here and no deck to pull from.

If this is our fate and nothing more than a nightmare, I won't allow anything to stop me from telling Tony how I feel before it's all ripped away from us.

I gaze up at his brown bedroom eyes and smile. "Tony, I think I love you."

Tony squeezes my thigh and draws me closer to him. "I think I love you too, Mia."

The End

Other Books by this Author.

The Prickling
The Unnerving
Sidero
The Carpenter's Chameleon-Book Two of Sidero

A special thanks to Dawn Angels, admin of the Facebook group Psychological Thriller Authors and Readers Unite. Your unwavering support of indie authors is appreciated.

-Dedicated to all the victims of domestic violence.